Brogan: Blood Money

L.D. TETLOW

A Black Horse Western

ROBERT HALE · LONDON

© L.D. Tetlow 1995
First published in Great Britain 1995

ISBN 0 7090 5537 4

Robert Hale Limited
Clerkenwell House
Clerkenwell Green
London EC1R 0HT

Photoset in North Wales by
Derek Doyle & Associates, Mold, Clwyd.
Printed and bound in Great Britain by
WBC Book Manufacturers Limited, Bridgend,
Mid-Glamorgan.

Brogan: Blood Money

ONE

Brogan McNally watched with a seemingly uninterested air as the three men, covered with the dust which showed many days of travelling through the desert, rode into town. However, his apparent indifference hid a sense of foreboding. He had seen these men before in various guises and in every case his instincts had proved correct, trouble of one kind or another had always ensued.

He did not know these particular men, but he knew the type, hard, mean and cruel. If they followed form, their priorities would be a drink and a woman in that order and, when they had satisfied these two basic instincts, they would be looking round to see if anyone dared to challenge their right to do exactly as they pleased.

From years of experience gained by his aimless drifting, he also knew that it was highly unlikely that anyone in town would seek to prevent their excesses. Most would simply find that they had other work out of town which required urgent attention or they would lock themselves and their families in their homes and hope that the men would soon grow tired of inaction and move on.

Sometimes this strategy worked but just occasionally it did not.

Brogan himself had ridden into town the
previous day and had intended continuing his
wanderings that day, after stocking up on a few
items which even he considered essential,
although he did try to avoid towns wherever
possible.

The small town of Spencer had appeared
harmless enough, situated at a ford across a river
which seemed to support a few farms along its
banks. Apart from farming there did not appear to
be much else. The sheriff, one Matt Fry, had eyed
Brogan with a slightly jaundiced eye but had not
made any attempt to move him on. Being moved
on was something Brogan was well accustomed to
and normally he simply obeyed instructions and
moved on. Very occasionally, particularly if a
sheriff proved too belligerent, he would rebel and
deliberately outstay his welcome. In the end
though he always left town.

There were, on the odd occasion, other reasons
why Brogan McNally, professional saddle tramp,
would stick his ground and at that precise
moment he had the distinct feeling that three of
those reasons had just entered Spencer.

It was not that Brogan ever looked for trouble;
in fact he usually tried to avoid it, but he had two
traits which he knew one day might very well
prove his undoing. The first was that he was
basically a rather nosy person, he could not help
but poke his nose into other people's affairs even
when it was made plain that he was not welcome.

The second was that he had an inherent sense of justice, although quite why this was so he could never really understand.

In this instance, Brogan's senses told him that someone in the town of Spencer was bound to suffer at the hands of these men. He based this assumption on two basic facts. The first was simply the men themselves, the word 'trouble' exuded from every movement they made, and the second was that Spencer was one of those rare towns which did not support the usual bar-girls in the saloon. Once these men had made that discovery they would be out and taking the first woman they fancied.

As the men dismounted and hitched their horses in front of a water trough, Brogan idly rose from his comfortable position under the shade of a tree and wandered the few yards to the sheriff's office, where Matt Fry was looking quite worried.

'Know 'em?' asked Brogan.

'Never seen 'em before in my life,' replied Matt, slowly shaking his head. 'I know who they are though, Clancy Jones, Mick Hobday and Onions Grimaldi.'

'Onions?' queried Brogan, unsure if he had heard correctly.

'That's what they call him,' sighed Matt. 'Onions on account of he always stinks of onions. Apparently he eats 'em raw, all the time. They say he's an Italian or somethin'. I guess that explains the onions; I hear they eat 'em all the time.'

'I wouldn't know about that,' admitted Brogan. 'The last Italian I came across, a mighty good-lookin' woman too, stank of garlic. Mind you, she said I just stank.'

Matt Fry sniffed and grinned slightly. 'She ain't wrong in that,' he said. 'Don't you ever take a bath?'

'Bathin' ain't healthy!' grunted Brogan. 'How come you know who they are?'

Matt nodded back into the office. 'I got their posters pinned up. All three wanted dead or alive for murder, bank robbery, arson an' rape. You name it seems they've done it.'

'So, here's your chance to make a name for yourself,' grinned Brogan. 'Just think of it, all the big papers back East carryin' the headlines "Matt Fry, Sheriff of Spencer, rids society of three hardened outlaws!" You could be really famous.'

Matt Fry grunted and looked down at his overlarge belly. 'Me, a hero? Do I look the hero type? Mr McNally, I like my job and I like it here in Spencer. I deal with the odd drunk, the occasional mad dog an', once in a while, we get a nice juicy domestic disturbance. Do you know when we last had a killin' in this town?' Brogan shook his head. 'Twelve years ago, that's how long an' even that warn't nothin' special. A young buck got too much drink inside him an' went wild with a rifle. He didn't intend killin' nobody; it was just plain bad luck old Stan got in the way.'

'Young buck?' queried Brogan. In his experience that was a phrase usually reserved for young Indians.

'Yeh, off the reserve,' confirmed Matt. 'We didn't deal with him, that was left to the Indian Affairs

Office an' his own people. I hear his own folk was pretty hard with him but I never did find out what happened to him.'

'Don't you ever get folk like these three through?'

'Sometimes,' grunted Matt. 'Up to now they've always left without doin' nothin', specially when they find out we don't have no cat-house in town.'

'Not even one whore in the saloon?' asked Brogan. 'Ain't you never had none?'

'A couple of girls did try settin' up once, maybe five years ago, but they was marched out of town within two days.'

Brogan laughed. 'Hell, I ain't never heard of men runnin' whores out of town before.'

'Who said anythin' about men?' grinned Matt. 'They was marched out at the head of a column of about forty women!'

'That I can understand!' Brogan laughed again. 'Spencer seems a nice kind of town, I'd hate to see it get torn apart by men like them. Don't you intend to do nothin'?'

'Not a damned thing just so long as they don't cause no trouble,' replied Matt, 'an' even if they do, I might just be out fishin' somewheres.'

'If they're as bad as you say, they must be worth a good bit in reward money,' said Brogan.

'Ten thousand dollars,' said Matt. 'Four thousand for Clancy Jones an' three thousand each the other two.'

Brogan whistled softly. 'A man could do things with that kind of money.'

'Includin' me,' admitted Matt, 'but I ain't about

to tempt fate. No money is any use if I'm dead.' He looked down at Brogan's gun. 'From the way you're wearin' that piece of ironmongery, I'd say you was a man who knew how to handle it. I reckon even you could find a good use for that much money.'

Brogan laughed. 'Sure, I reckon I could find a use for it, but I'll probably end up givin' it away to some deservin' cause or other. The truth is I just don't have no need for that much, especially when you start talkin' in numbers I can hardly understand. All I need is enough to get by, pay my way, buy a few supplies an' a few bullets. I just don't need no more.'

'You could settle down an' find yourself a good woman,' suggested Matt.

'Me, settle down with a woman!' exclaimed Brogan. 'Hell, man, you'll be suggestin' I have a bath next!'

Matt Fry laughed. 'Guess not. Can't say as I blame you either. At least you don't have no worries.'

'I gets my share,' assured Brogan. 'Right now I'm worried just what's goin' to happen when them three find out there ain't no women available.'

'You're worried!' grunted Matt. 'Why the hell should that concern you? All you've got to do is get on that flea-bitten horse of yours an' ride out of town. After that, what happens here is no concern of yours at all.'

'I could do exactly that,' agreed Brogan, 'but I guess you could say I just can't mind my own business though.'

Matt Fry looked strangely at the saddle tramp.

'Funny, I wouldn't've figured you for a man who would go lookin' for trouble.'

'I don't,' said Brogan, 'it just sorta happens to me. Anyhow, I reckon that's 'cos you know I'm a saddlebum an' up to now all the saddlebums you've met have been only too willin' to steal candy from a baby an' run like hell as soon as any sign of trouble appears.'

'Somethin' like that!' agreed Matt.

'Well this particular saddlebum ain't like any other you've ever met. Although I says so myself, I'm honest; I ain't never stole nothin' from nobody; I ain't never murdered nobody an' I know how to handle myself an' a gun.'

Matt Fry nodded. 'I already checked you out, McNally, that was the first thing I did as soon as you rode in. It's the first thing I do as soon as any stranger rides in. You're unusual; as far as I can tell there ain't nothin' out on you at all. In my book that makes you someone to watch out for. You wear your gun just like other professional gunslingers I've met, an' I've met a few an' although you reckon you ain't never murdered nobody – an' I believe you – I reckon you an' death are no strangers. I'd say there's quite a few men had cause to regret ever gettin' on the wrong side of you.'

Brogan smiled slightly and nodded. 'I've killed my share of men, more than most people like me have ever done. I can't say as I'm proud of it, but I sure as hell ain't ashamed either. Whatever men I have killed have always been in self-defence or in defence of someone else.'

Matt nodded sagely. 'I can believe that. I can read most men like a book. That's why I didn't run you out of town yesterday. Some folk wanted me to, they don't like their town an' their lives bein' cluttered up with stinkin' saddle tramps. I had you figured for just passin' through an' a man who wouldn't be too easily scared.'

'An' how do you read them three?' Brogan nodded in the direction of the men now entering the only saloon in Spencer.

'Like you do,' muttered Matt. 'Trouble. Trouble with a capital T. I can only hope they decide Spencer ain't worth the bother an' ride out, but somethin' tells me that ain't about to happen.'

'Still goin' fishin'?' asked Brogan.

'Just let me find my fishin' pole!' grunted Matt, returning inside his office.

As Brogan had expected and almost confidently predicted, the entire population of Spencer had suddenly discovered they had unfinished business somewhere. About thirty seconds after the three outlaws entered the saloon, seven men scurried out, two to leap astride their horses and gallop out of town and the other five to head for their homes where they shuttered every window. The few children who had been playing in the street miraculously vanished into thin air and two lone women remounted the buckboard they had ridden into town on and disappeared in a cloud of dust down the trail by the river. It seemed that apart from the three outlaws, one small yapping dog and a cat who looked in disdain at the antics of the dog, Brogan McNally was the only person still in town. Brogan smiled to himself and slowly wandered across the street to the saloon.

'You is completely mad!' he said to himself. 'Where the hell do you think you're goin'?'

'The saloon,' he replied to himself.

Talking aloud to himself was quite normal to Brogan, especially when he was trying to justify what was a seemingly irrational and stupid action on his part. Sometimes he would talk to his horse and she seemed to understand his every word and meaning. He had to admit that most times the horse made more sense than he did. He found that talking either to himself or his horse helped to sort things out.

'An' just what the hell are you gonna do?'

'How the hell do I know that? It all depends on what they do. I ain't no mind reader.'

'One of these days you ain't goin' to have no mind to do anythin' with,' he scolded himself. 'Someone's goin' to blow it away with your brains, what brains you do have.'

'It ain't happened yet!' he replied, simply.

Having satisfied himself with that last point, Brogan did as he always did and ignored his own good advice and went into the saloon. He was not sure who was more surprised to see him, the outlaws or the bartender.

'Beer,' Brogan called, marching up to the counter. He nodded at the three outlaws, smiled slightly and handed over a coin in return for the beer drawn by a very mystified bartender. He took a long drink and slowly turned slightly to look at the three outlaws. They too seemed rather mystified and even a little worried.

In their experience men simply did not remain in the same room as them. The reaction of the previous seven occupants had been predictable and Clancy Jones, Mick Hobday and Onions Grimaldi enjoyed it when things happened as they thought they should. The arrival of this saddle tramp rather upset their equilibrium.

'Long ride?' asked Brogan. 'I seen you ride in. By the state of you I'd say you just come across the desert.'

'What's it to do with you?' growled Clancy Jones.

'Precisely nothin',' agreed Brogan. 'Just makin' conversation, that's all.'

'Supposin' we don't want no conversation?' grated Mick Hobday.

'Well, that's about all you is gonna get in this town,' said Brogan. 'Good beer an' maybe good conversation. Mind, the quality of the conversation depends on how good you is at talkin', talkin' sense that is. You've probably found out already that there ain't no women to be had.'

Clancy Jones looked enquiringly at the bartender, Sam, who nodded and gulped slightly.

'He's right, we don't have no bar-girls in here an' whores ain't allowed in town. The womenfolk see to it that women like that ain't welcome.'

'Don't you men have no say in the matter?'

'Not a lot,' admitted Sam. 'For the most part what our womenfolk say is almost law. Anyhow, we ain't got no need. We don't have no ranches so we don't get no cowboys an' apart from you an' him....' He nodded at Brogan. 'We haven't had no strangers through here in over three weeks.'

'You're a stranger too!' hissed Onions Grimaldi. 'From the way you are talkin' I thought you was livin' here.'

'Like you, just passin' through,' said Brogan. 'Man, believe me, this is one town which is well worth just passin' through.'

'We'll decide if a town's worth passin' through or not,' grunted Mick Hobday. 'We don't need no saddlebum to give us no advice.'

'That obvious is it,' laughed Brogan, 'me bein' a saddlebum?'

'You stink just like they all do!' snarled Clancy Jones.

Brogan made an exaggerated show of screwing up his nose and sniffing the air. 'You three don't exactly smell of roses either!'

'Meanin'?' threatened Onions Grimaldi.

'Meanin' just that,' said Brogan, taking another gulp at his beer and then sniffing again. 'Onions! Yeh that's it, that's what stinks around here.' He looked at the bartender and smiled. 'You cookin' onions, Sam?'

The bartender shuffled uneasily and pretended to busy himself by drying already dry glasses. He looked at the three outlaws and then at Brogan as if uncertain who was going to be the more trouble. He finally decided that perhaps the dirty saddle tramp was probably the more dangerous.

'Look, Mr ... er ...' he faltered.

'McNally!' smiled Brogan. 'Brogan McNally, just call me Brogan.'

'McNally ...' said Sam. 'Look, McNally, we run a peaceful town here, we don't need the likes of you causin' trouble....'

'Me cause trouble!' exclaimed Brogan. 'All I'm doin' is samplin' your very excellent beer. Since when has somethin' like that been trouble?'

Sam shot a glance at the outlaws and seemed lost for words. Eventually he found his tongue again. 'There's nothin' in Spencer for any of you. We ain't got no bank, no assay office; in fact nothin' that could interest men like you at all.'

'Suits me fine!' grinned Brogan. 'Now, back to that onion smell. I know where it's comin' from, it's you....' He nodded at Grimaldi. 'Yeh, it figures. Onions Grimaldi, three thousand, dead or alive!'

Suddenly all three men were going for their guns but Brogan had anticipated just such a reaction and before they could draw their guns they were staring into the barrel of Brogan's Colt. Brogan did not shoot but simply grinned knowingly at them.

'Who's gonna be first?' he invited.

Clancy Jones was the first to release his gun, although he was clearly very annoyed at being outdrawn by some unknown saddlebum. The other two gave Clancy a brief glance before they too allowed their guns to drop back into their holsters.

'Very fancy!' sneered Clancy Jones. 'OK, this time you got the drop on us. From now on, McNally – or whatever your name is – you'd better make sure you got eyes up your ass 'cos next time you won't get the chance to outdraw anybody.'

'I was born with eyes up my ass!' said Brogan, slipping his gun back. 'That's somethin' you'd better believe. You'd also better believe I can shoot a fly off a wall from twenty yards.'

'OK, Mr Wise-Guy,' said Clancy Jones. 'You've proved your point, what else is it you want, why this show of bravado?'

'Just invitin' you to leave town peaceful like,' said Brogan. 'I ain't interested in who you are or what you done. I know your names, Clancy Jones, Mick Hobday an' Onions Grimaldi. I also know you're worth ten thousand between you, which is very temptin' I've got to admit, but I ain't no bounty hunter. Like Sam says, this is a peaceful town an' I agree with him that it don't need folk like you messin' it up. You leave now, quietly, an' that'll be the end of the matter.'

'An' if we don't?' challenged Mick Hobday.

Brogan shrugged. 'Then maybe I'd better get the town undertaker to measure you all up for boxes.'

'Big words, McNally,' hissed Onions Grimaldi. 'Right now we got a US marshal an' two deputy marshals hot on our trail. We reckon they're about three days behind.'

'Interestin',' mused Brogan. 'So what?'

'The so what is,' said Clancy Jones, 'if you think we're trouble, just you wait until Marshal Fox arrives. The only similarity between him an' the law is that he wears a badge. He don't give a toss who gets in his way, women or children, I seen him kill both an' not bat an eye.'

'I don't see how that should affect me or this town,' said Brogan.

Clancy Jones laughed. 'For a start he don't like

sheriffs what run when the likes of us is about. He's even been known to shoot a couple of sheriffs for doin' just that. Marshal Fox, a good name 'cos he's just as cunnin' as a fox.'

'So if he's so close on your trail, why the hell don't you just ride on out?' suggested Brogan.

'Three dead-beat horses!' explained Hobday. 'We was goin' to change 'em here, but we had a look round 'fore we came in an' it don't look like anybody's got any decent animals. All folk seem to have is work horses.'

'Hardly surprisin' in farmin' country,' said Brogan.

'Maybe not,' said Jones. 'If there had been decent horses we'd've been gone by now, but, as it is, we got to risk restin' our horses for a while. In the meantime, we just thought we'd have us some fun with some poor farmer's lady.'

'Yeh,' agreed Grimaldi. 'That was what we decided, but I'd say we've got a better game right now, it's called hunt McNally!'

Brogan laughed and decided to leave the saloon. 'Good huntin'!' he called as the door swung behind him.

TWO

Sheriff Matt Fry almost cowered at the back of his office as Brogan burst through the door, as if he had been expecting the outlaws. His look of relief was plain when he saw Brogan.

'I never expected to see you alive again,' he said, rather nervously and with a weak grin. 'I thought you was completely mad to go in the saloon.'

'That's what most folk think,' said Brogan, 'includin' them. It kinda knocks 'em off balance when folk don't react like they think they ought to. Anyhow, I proved one thing, to myself at least, they ain't so hot on the draw, I outdrew 'em easier'n I could've outdrawn some kid.'

'You … you outdrew 'em!' Matt looked incredulous. 'I didn't hear no shootin'!'

'That's 'cos there wasn't none,' laughed Brogan. 'I just outdrew 'em, that's all. Anyhow, that ain't what I came to tell you. It seems there's a marshal an' two deputies on their trail, they reckon about three days behind. Some feller by the name of Fox. You ever heard of him?'

It was quite obvious that Matt Fry had heard of Marshal Fox. What bit of colour there had been in his face drained and his eyes stared wildly.

'God help us!' he exclaimed. 'I think I'd rather face them three out there than have him in town.'

'That's what they said,' said Brogan. 'Who the hell is this feller? If he's a lawman surely there ain't no need for law-abidin' folk to be scared of him.'

'Don't you believe it!' groaned Matt. 'Before he was made a marshal, Ebenezer Fox was a bounty hunter, probably the best bounty hunter there ever was. He's ruthless, cunnin' an' damned clever an' he don't care who gets in his way. In fact he was so good they decided to make him a marshal, just to make everythin' he does all legal like, save havin' to answer a lot of difficult questions. He ain't like other marshals though, he refused a salary, instead they agreed that he an' his men take any reward money they earn. It seems to be an arrangement that suits both the authorities an' him.'

'In other words he's nothin' more than a killer hired by the country,' said Brogan.

'That's about as close as you can get to it,' agreed Matt. 'Three days! Christ, I hope to hell they've gone by then.'

'They reckon he kills sheriffs what run out,' said Brogan, goading the sheriff somewhat.

'That too!' admitted Matt. 'So it looks like I got the choice of runnin' an' risk bein' shot by Fox or stayin' an' risk bein' killed by them.'

'You could kill them,' suggested Brogan.

Matt Fry stared at Brogan for a moment and then suddenly laughed nervously. 'That kind of thing is strictly for the birds an' mad dogs.'

'In the meantime they'll be demandin' a woman apiece,' reminded Brogan. 'Are you just goin' to stand aside an' let 'em?'

'What the hell do you expect me to do?' rasped Matt. 'Sorry, but it's a case of every man for himself as far as I'm concerned, I resign here an' now!' He ripped his badge of office from the front of his shirt and threw it on the table. He also threw a bunch of keys alongside the badge. 'Now, where's my fishin' pole? I'm off to bag me a big catfish I got staked out!'

He did not wait for Brogan to say anything, simply barging past him and out into the street. Brogan watched, almost amused, from the doorway as Matt Fry stormed off down the street. He saw him stop and talk to a couple of people, waving his arms in an agitated fashion and pointing to his office. A short while later, while Brogan was still wondering if he ought to tell anyone, three well-dressed men approached the office.

'Mr McNally?' asked the leader of the men, turning his head slightly as he caught scent of Brogan's unsavoury body odours. Brogan nodded, already knowing what the man was about to say. 'Mr McNally,' continued the man, 'I'm James Watson, Mayor of Spencer....' He turned to the man behind his left shoulder. 'This is Pete Green, the town's lawyer and this....' He indicated the man on his right. 'This is Amos Smith, a member of the town council.' Brogan nodded at each in turn as they went through into the office.

The lawyer, Pete Green, picked up the sheriff's

badge and the bunch of keys and nervously played with them. 'It would appear that we are without a sheriff,' he said.

'Quite,' said James Watson. 'That is what we have come to talk to you about, Mr McNally....'

'No thanks!' laughed Brogan.

'No thanks to what?' asked the lawyer. 'We haven't said anything yet.'

'No, but you're goin' to,' said Brogan. 'You just lost your sheriff on account of he's shit scared of three outlaws an' a marshal an' you want someone to protect you.'

'Well ... er ... yes, I suppose you could put it like that, Mr McNally. It would appear that this town is in need of the services of a sheriff....'

'What did you say about Matt Fry runnin' scared of a marshal?' asked Amos Smith.

'Just that,' smiled Brogan. 'It seems them three men in the saloon is bein' tailed by some marshal by the name of Fox, Ebenezer Fox, or somethin' like that.'

The three councillors looked nervously at each other and shuffled uneasily. 'Do you know Marshal Fox?' asked the lawyer.

'Never heard of him till now,' admitted Brogan.

'But you do know he's headed this way?' pressed the lawyer.

'You know as much as I do,' said Brogan.

'Quite!' muttered the mayor. 'However, the point is that we are, at this moment, in urgent need of a sheriff. Under the circumstances we feel that you would be an ideal candidate for the job, Mr McNally.'

'Ideal candidate!' exclaimed Brogan. 'Sure, I was a sheriff once, not for long though, so you could say I've got some experience, but that's somethin' you couldn't know. In fact you know absolutely nothin' about me, so what makes me so ideal?'

'Well ... well,' faltered the mayor. 'There was a witness as to what happened in the saloon between you an' those outlaws. We hear you are very fast with that gun of yours and apparently not afraid to use it.'

'Witness?' asked Brogan. 'I didn't see no witness.'

'Probably not,' said Amos Smith. 'It was pure chance really. Bart Wills was being his usual nosy self, looking through a crack in the back door and he saw what happened. He came runnin' to to tell us. It would appear that the town needs someone like you.'

Brogan laughed loudly. 'I'll tell you why this town needs someone like me. It's 'cos you don't know me, you owe me nothin' so it won't matter none if I just happen to get myself killed. All you're lookin' for is a scapegoat, someone to sacrifice if need be. Sorry, gentlemen, I don't like the terms, I'm a loner an' I don't owe this town nothin' just like it don't owe me nothin'. You want a sheriff, I suggest you go find someone else or persuade Matt Fry to take his badge back.'

'Five dollars a week an' all found!' offered the mayor.

'An' hope that I don't live to collect!' sneered Brogan.

'Seven dollars!' interjected the lawyer.

Brogan laughed and spat on the floor. 'Go shit on your seven dollars! Anyhow, I'm a loner, I've been wanderin' all my life an' I can't see me settlin' down now.'

'Ten!' exclaimed the mayor. 'That's the absolute maximum we can got to.'

'Not for a thousand a week,' said Brogan. 'Sorry, gentlemen, no deal. Now, if you don't mind, I think it's about time I was on my way. I ain't got no quarrel with them three outlaws, I can't see 'em botherin' about me.'

Actually, Brogan could not have been more wrong. Almost as soon as he had walked out of the saloon, the three outlaws had been planning just how they were going to deal with the saddle tramp.

The one thing they were in agreement with was that Brogan was obviously too dangerous to be tackled head on. While they agreed that if all three faced him and he was only likely to be able to kill one of them, they were definitely not agreed upon who that one should be. In the end it came down to the well-established method of shooting their victim in the back. Exactly when and where did not matter, they would do so just as soon as the opportunity presented itself.

Brogan too was not quite so certain about his assertions, but he was not prepared to tell the councillors, mainly because of his own pride. It was always possible that the outlaws would simply allow him to ride out of town but, through experience of such men, he thought it most unlikely. He had dented what pride they had by outdrawing them in the saloon and they would not forget too easily.

However, he decided to test their resolve and attempt to leave town so, on leaving the sheriff's office, he wandered slowly towards the stables, all the time keeping a watchful ear and eye open. His caution was not a waste of time as he caught a glimpse of one of the outlaws watching him from through the window of the saloon. As he walked, Brogan made an accurate mental picture of the layout and buildings adjacent to the saloon, since this was the direction he intended to go.

He paid his bill – one dollar – at the stable, saddled his horse and then checked his rifle. He had purchased what supplies he needed earlier and these were either stowed in his saddle-bags or slung across his saddle. The owner of the stable did not hang about to make conversation as such men usually did, he just grabbed the money and disappeared.

'You ready for trouble, old girl?' he asked his horse. She snorted and shook her head. 'No? You've had it too easy for too long,' continued Brogan. 'You're gettin' lazy.' This time the horse nodded her head vigorously. 'Well, all I can say is you be ready to run like you've never run before when I says so!' The horse looked at him wide eyed and snorted again. Brogan laughed. 'You just do as you're told or else I might trade you in for a younger horse.' This time she turned and butted him with her nose. 'OK, OK,' he grinned. 'I was only jokin'!'

Brogan and his horse had been together for almost as long as he could remember and they seemed to have struck up something of an understanding – both of them thought he was completely mad on occasion.

Rather than ride out of the stable, Brogan led his horse. The purpose of this was to allow himself more time in observing any tell-tale signs further up the street. As before, the street was completely deserted apart from the same small dog he had seen earlier. The mayor, the lawyer and the other town councillor were still inside the sheriff's office. This was confirmed when he saw a face peering through the grimy window staring at him.

The outlaws were more noticeable by their absence than their presence and Brogan knew that they must be lying in wait for him somewhere. He had given them plenty of time to see that he was leaving and at the very least he would have expected them to jeer or cat-call at him from the boardwalk in front of the saloon. Since this was seemingly not going to happen, he had to assume the worst.

Actually it was the small dog which gave away the position of one of the outlaws, at least Brogan had to assume that it was one of them and not the cat which had attracted the dog's attention earlier. The dog was standing at the corner of a narrow alleyway opposite the saloon, wagging its stump of a tail and looking up expectantly. The presence of someone in the alley seemed confirmed when the dog suddenly yelped and ran away.

Brogan slowly mounted, all the time watching and listening. He nudged his horse forward, moving to the side of the street opposite the saloon, noting a brief flash of what appeared to be a face in the window of the saloon and the small dog's sudden interest in something underneath the boardwalk. Once again the dog seemed to have been scared away. He smiled to himself, he was now quite satisfied that all three outlaws had been accounted for, one in the alleyway, one under the boardwalk and one inside the saloon.

Casually, and to the average eye too casually, Brogan slung his rifle across his arms as his horse, with seeming practised and measured tread, plodded onward. He passed the sheriff's office and smilingly acknowledged the three men inside. The faces suddenly disappeared in confusion. From that point onward his eyes darted from alleyway to boardwalk to saloon, trying to work out where the first shot would come from.

Suddenly he screamed at his old horse to 'go!', which with surprisingly swift turn of foot she did. This unexpected activity took the waiting outlaws completely off their guard; The saloon window smashed, the man in the alleyway suddenly appeared and a grimy face showed itself under the boardwalk.

Things had happened quickly, which was as Brogan intended. His horse was almost flying up the street as the first shot echoed around. Suddenly the horse was riderless as Brogan flung himself from the saddle to land, quite painfully he had to admit afterwards, behind the water trough outside the saloon and among the flailing hooves of the outlaws' horses.

Brogan's first shot was into the terrified face of the man underneath the boardwalk, not more than ten feet away. There was no need for a second shot! He knew he had chosen well, the now panicking horses gave him perfect cover, although he did wince a few times as hooves crashed down on his body.

He pulled himself into a crouching position, managed a brief glimpse of the man in the alleyway – Onion Grimaldi – aimed and fired. That shot did not kill Onions; he staggered, clutching at his shoulder and in so doing presented a full target. Brogan's second shot made Onions Grimaldi forget all about the pain in his arm. Suddenly there was silence, even the horses calmed down.

Brogan looked between the legs of the horses, listened for any sounds on the boardwalk and then waited. He smiled to himself knowing that whoever was in the saloon was also playing a waiting game. It was now just a matter of who would give first and Brogan knew that it was not going to be him.

'Looks like there's just the two of us!' called Brogan.

'An' pretty soon there'll be just the one of us!' came the response. 'Me!'

'Not if I can help it!' replied Brogan, straining to see the now shattered window of the saloon. From where he was his view was greatly impeded by the three horses and he had to stand up, using one of the horses as cover, to be able to see into the dim interior of the saloon. There was nobody to be seen which told Brogan that he was being approached from a different direction. The faintest of creaks from the boardwalk to his left, slightly behind him told him everything else he needed to know.

There was only one shot, that was all that was needed as the body of Clancy Jones twisted and arched before slumping over the rail and finally ending up in an untidy heap half on and half off the boardwalk. Brogan slowly moved out from cover, forever careful just in case one of the outlaws should still be alive and still prepared to fight. In the event all three were very dead.

Sam was the first to show, looking at the body of Clancy Jones, scratching his head and turning his attention to seemingly more important matters, his broken window.

'Have you got any idea how long it takes to get a piece of glass that size?' he muttered. 'I got to send all the way to Nelson City for somethin' like that.'

'Could've been worse,' grinned Brogan. 'You could've been dead.'

'Naw,' said Sam in a very matter-of-fact manner, 'nobody ever shoots a bartender, they just ain't worth the bother.'

Brogan smiled and considered. He had to admit that in all his wandering and all the killings he had witnessed, he had never yet seen a bartender murdered, not that he could remember.

'The other one's under the boardwalk,' said Brogan, pointing with his rifle. 'Pretty messy too, he took it full in the face.'

'It ain't his problem no more,' grunted Sam. He looked down the street and gave a derisive snort, which reminded Brogan that he had to recover his horse. 'Here they come, the three wise men. Just like Matt Fry, tryin' to look all important once everythin' sorted out. By the way, what happened to Matt?'

'Decided to leave his badge an' take up fishin',' said Brogan, smiling at the now purposeful and important manner of the three councillors as they drew near.

'I ain't surprised,' said Sam. 'Good man really, providin' the most he had to deal with was a drunk now an' then. Trouble is this town has had it too easy for too long. Folk hardly know how to use a gun these days, it's been so long since they had cause to.'

'I'd say that was a good thing,' said Brogan.

'Probably you're right,' admitted Sam. 'It's just that when somethin' does happen we don't know what the hell to do.'

'Will you know what to do when this Marshal Ebernezer Fox hits town?' asked Brogan.

'Me?' laughed Sam. 'Sure, I'll know exactly what to do, let 'em have all they want to drink on the house. It's them three you should be askin' that. I sure hope they got plenty of clean underwear 'cos when Fox does hit, they're sure gonna do some shittin' in their pants!' He laughed coarsely and acknowledged the councillors as they stepped up on to the boardwalk.

'Er ... I ... er ... we ...' faltered the mayor, the purpose and certainty of their approach suddenly evaporating as they faced Brogan. 'We … er … we saw what happened and....'

'I very much doubt if you saw a damned thing,' sneered Brogan. 'You was all too busy shittin' yourselves.' He sniffed the air. 'I guess I ain't the only one what stinks now.'

'The point is,' said the lawyer, Pete Green, 'you have just killed three men. We agree they were all wanted men with rewards out on them but....'

'But nothin'!' hissed Brogan. 'They was out to kill me so I killed them instead. You're a lawyer, you ought to know it's what they call self-defence.'

'Quite possibly, Mr McNally,' agreed the mayor, 'but we don't have much experience of these matters in this town. We have little doubt that you did act in self-defence, but we have to be certain of the law....'

'Mister!' snarled Brogan suddenly drawing his Colt and pressing the barrel into Mayor Watson's nostril, making the man whimper and almost stand on his toes. 'There's only one thing you've got to be certain of an' that's this!' He thrust the gun, making Watson stand on his toes again and whimper more loudly. 'Just in case you've forgot, this is called a gun an' if I squeeze this trigger, it goes off bang, an' if it goes off bang right now, the top of your head gets blown off. I don't know just what any of you is tryin' to prove, but I'd forget any fancy ideas you do have. I was goin' to leave town, but I got to thinkin' about the reward money out on these three. I reckon I can put ten thousand to good use.'

'Quite!' Mayor Watson breathed easier as

Brogan holstered his gun. He rubbed his nose and sniffed.'Quite!' he repeated. 'I would agree that you are perfectly entitled to the reward. However, we do not have the means to pay you, besides which we don't know what the procedure is....'

'Then you'd better ask Marshal Ebenezer Fox,' said Brogan. 'If they was right, he should be here in a couple of days, maybe three. He'll know what to do.'

'Marshal Fox has something of a reputation,' said the lawyer, Green; 'he apparently makes his living by collecting rewards. I don't suppose he is going to be too pleased at you collecting instead of him.'

Brogan laughed. 'I've gotta admit, that's the main reason I decided to take the reward. If I was to leave this marshal to it, he'd probably claim the reward for himself, knowin' full well that you'd all be too scared to say anythin' about it. I have this objection to other folk gainin' by my effort.'

The three councillors looked nervously at each other before Mayor Watson spoke. 'As far as we are concerned that is not our problem. You will have to sort out any problems between yourselves. The only thing we can say is we hope you do it well away from this town.'

'I'll just play things as they come,' said Brogan. 'In the meantime, what was that you was sayin' about havin' to be sure about the law ...?'

'Quite!' said Mayor Watson. It was a word he used frequently, even too frequently for his fellow councillors' liking on occasion. This time however they raised no objection.

Brogan laughed and wandered off up the street to bring his old horse back.

THREE

Later that day, Matt Fry showed his face in town and seemed rather worried when almost the first person he saw was Brogan. He grinned weakly and held up three fair-sized catfish.

'Couldn't catch the big one, he's too wily.'

'It's OK,' said Brogan with some iron in his voice. 'There ain't no danger no more. Jones, Hobday an' Grimaldi are all dead. You can have your safe little town back now.'

'Yeh, well ... I guess so. It warn't that I was scared....'

'Sure, Matt,' smiled Brogan, 'you don't have to do no explainin' to me, I don't matter, I ain't nobody. Mind, I could've been. The dust had hardly settled behind your butt before that mayor of yours an' that lawyer were round offerin' me your job.'

'They did?' Matt seemed rather upset at the news. 'You didn't take it though?'

'What the hell do I want to be a sheriff for?' said Brogan. 'I tried it once but it just ain't my scene. I reckon you've only got to pin that badge back on an' everything'll be back to how it always was.'

'You reckon?' Matt seemed somewhat relieved. Then he frowned and shook his head. 'Ebenezer Fox! I reckon he'll be here soon an' he's one lawman I just do not fancy tanglin' with. I reckon the town can do without my services a mite longer. It looks like I'm goin' to spend me a few days fishin'.'

'You'd better tell 'em that yourself,' smiled Brogan, 'they're headin' right this way!'

Matt had no time to avoid the trio of councillors and Brogan left him to explain his actions. From that point onward Matt Fry was very noticeable by his absence. Later still that day, Brogan was once again offered the position of sheriff and once again he refused.

The news of Marshal Ebenezer Fox's impending arrival in Spencer preceeded the actual event by about four hours. He and his two surly-looking deputies arrived in town a couple of hours before sunset and, much to the chagrin of Mayor Watson, Lawyer Green and Councillor Amos Smith, ignored them completely and stomped into the saloon.

The three members of the council had decided to form a small reception committee, hoping somehow to gain some sort of influence over the marshal. It seemed that Marshal Fox had seen it all before and barely hid his contempt. In some confusion the councillors followed the marshal into the saloon.

There appeared to be no question of Marshal Fox or his men paying for their drinks, at least not on their part and Sam, true to his word, was prepared to supply it free. He did not extend the same courtesy to the three councillors, holding out his hand for their money.

'Er ... Marshal Fox!' said Mayor Watson. 'I am the mayor of Spencer and....'

'Who killed 'em?' demanded Fox.

'I ... er ... I beg your pardon?' said the mayor, rather taken aback at the abruptness.

'You heard well enough!' grated Fox. 'I said who killed 'em?'

'You mean Jones, Hobday an' Grimaldi?' said the mayor.

'Is everyone else in this God-forsaken town as thick as their mayor?' snapped Fox. 'Who the hell else could I mean?'

'Not us!' exclaimed Lawyer Green. 'We didn't have nothin' to do with it.'

Fox laughed and then sneered. 'No, sir, I don't expect you did. Your type never have anythin' to do with anythin' but you expect all the glory. Now answer the question. Who the hell killed 'em, surely you know that?'

'McNally!' croaked Amos Smith. 'Brogan McNally. He ain't nobody of any consequence, just a....'

'Nobody of no consequence!' laughed Fox. 'A man kills the most wanted men in the State, possibly the whole of the country an' you say he's of no consequence? I'd say he was a man of very great consequence as far as you're concerned. He didn't exactly just step on three cockroaches.'

'That's not what I ... we meant,' said Amos

Smith. 'He's just a saddle tramp who just happened to be here when they arrived. Our own sheriff was ... er ... indisposed at the time, in fact he still is, but we know that he would have handled the situation without any trouble.'

Once again Ebenezer Fox laughed loudly, this time joined by his deputies. 'Indisposed!' he laughed. 'Yeh, I guess he was. He wouldn't be the first sheriff I come across who's suddenly taken very ill an' I doubt he'll be the last. Scum, that's what men like that are. Seems like this saddle tramp wasn't afraid to use his gun though.' He thought for a moment. 'Strange that, all the saddle tramps I ever met have run like hell at the first sign of trouble, but I hear this one didn't.'

'Where did you hear that?' asked Green.

'Heard nothin' else ever since we hit the county,' said Fox. 'Seems like this saddle tramp has caused quite a stir. I hear that you ain't had anythin' like this in livin' memory.'

'We have been very fortunate in that respect,' said Mayor Watson. 'That's the way we'd prefer it to remain as well. Spencer may be a very quiet and uninteresting town to most folk passing through but it's plenty good enough for those of us who have to work and live here.'

Ebenezer Fox smiled and nodded. 'I ain't knockin' the town,' he said, 'I wish there were more places like it. Yep, a town like this is just the kind of place I'd choose to retire in. This saddle tramp interests me though. I think him an' me ought to have a few words an' get one or two things straight between us.'

'Quite!' muttered Mayor Watson. 'However, we feel we must point out that Mr McNally – Brogan, I believe he's called – does not seem to fit into the usual category of saddle tramps. Like most other towns, we get our share of such people passing through so we know the type....'

'A saddlebum is a saddlebum!' growled one of the deputies.

Mayor Watson flinched nervously. 'Quite! Under normal circumstances I would agree, but not in this case....'

'Where is he?' demanded the marshal.

'That I couldn't say,' said the mayor, almost apologetically.

Ebenezer Fox laughed derisively. 'You have a dangerous saddle tramp wanderin' about town an' you don't know where he is right now! I would have thought he was one man you would have wanted to know every movement of. I know I would in your case. I'd want to know every time he so much as farted, picked his nose or scratched his balls.'

'Quite!' apologized the mayor.

'An' if you say "Quite" one more time I'll personally shoot off your balls one at a time! I want to see this saddle tramp who's so different. We'll soon see just how different he really is.'

Mayor Watson choked as he almost repeated the offending word. 'I'll send someone out to find him,' he offered. 'He can't be far away, I believe his horse is still in the stables.'

'Do that!' growled the marshal. 'In the meantime we need somewhere to sleep the night. Does this place have any hotels?'

'I got a couple of rooms I let out,' said Sam, the bartender. 'Nice an' clean. You're more'n welcome to have them, no charge of course.'

'Mighty civil of you,' said Fox, 'don't mind if we do.'

'Up the stairs, first an' second on the right,' said Sam. 'If you're wantin' somethin' to eat though, I don't run to that. Maisie Fullwood down the street is the best eatin' place, in fact it's the only eatin' place.'

'That'll suit us fine,' said Fox. He turned to his deputies and ordered them to take their bags up to the rooms.

'I'll send out for McNally then!' said Mayor Watson.

Ebenezer Fox glared at him and then growled, 'I'd've thought you'd've done that by now!'

The mayor almost repeated the offensive word of 'Quite' but stopped himself just in time and looked about the saloon. Eventually his eyes lighted upon a lone, elderly man who was trying desperately to appear uninterested in what was happening but quite plainly failing.

'Gus,' said the mayor, 'go see if you can find McNally.'

Gus looked very alarmed and suddenly decided that he had far more important matters to attend to than run errands for the mayor. He muttered something about the mayor looking himself and ran from the saloon. The mayor looked at his companions and shrugged. By unspoken agreement all three left the saloon and began searching for Brogan, each in different directions.

*   *   *

In fact Brogan had witnessed the arrival of Marshal Ebenezer Fox and had laughed to himself at the antics of the self-appointed reception committee. He had watched as the marshal had simply ignored the three men and he could well imagine the scene inside the saloon.

Brogan prided himself in being able to form an instant and normally very accurate assessment of a man and his character and in the case of Marshal Ebenezer Fox, he had seen a single-minded man who was not prepared to be trifled with or fobbed off with platitudes or excuses. He also saw a very dangerous man to whom the prospect of sudden and violent death meant very little, even if that death were to be his own. He also had very little doubt that he was a man who could handle both himself and a gun extremely well. Here was a man to be very wary of.

The marshal's deputies too seemed to be men who needed careful handling and he quickly formed the opinion that they would follow instructions to the letter and be prepared to kill anyone or anything at a nod from their leader. All three men were all the more dangerous for the fact that they wore badges of office. He decided that they were little more than official murderers.

However, this assessment of the trio was not the reason Brogan had stayed out of their way. He knew very well that the marshal would be demanding to see him and since he had a natural resentment of men in power and authority, he had decided that he too would play the hard man. He was not prepared under any circumstances to show any sign of weakness or fear of the marshal or his deputies.

Fear never entered into things, Brogan simply did not have any fear of such things and, knowing that he would be summoned, he deliberately made himself scarce.

As he just happened to be rather hungry, he had decided to eat at Maisie Fullwood's. He had eaten there daily since he had been in Spencer and he and Maisie, a rather large and forbidding widow, had struck something of an understanding. It appeared that she too was not all that certain as to the virtues of hot water and soap and was one of the few people not to sniff whenever Brogan entered. She too seemed to know that the marshal would be demanding to see Brogan.

'Gus Morton just come runnin' out of the saloon like the devil himself was on his tail!' laughed Maisie as she placed a dish of steaming stew in front of Brogan. 'I reckon he was just told to go find you but he sure ain't lookin' too hard.'

'It was only a matter of time,' grinned Brogan. 'Someone else is sure to be lookin' for me soon an' it won't be the marshal or his men, they wouldn't lower 'emselves to do somethin' like that.'

'You're right about that!' laughed Maisie. 'Here they come now, the terrible threesome. You know, I reckon they must even shit together. I often wonder if they have extra wide beds just so's they can hump their wives together. Maybe they even share their women.'

'Are they lookin'?'

'Sure are!' grinned Maisie. 'Hell, that's one for the book, they even split up an' that's somethin' you don't see very often. Seems Marshal Fox has managed to uncouple them from each other's asses. The mayor is headed this way.'

'He can wait!' asserted Brogan.

Mayor Watson came up to the dingy window and peered inside and, on seeing the object of his search at a table, scurried inside breathlessly.

'You'd better come quick!' he panted. 'Marshal Fox is demandin' to see the man who killed the outlaws.'

'Can't you see I'm eatin'?' growled Brogan.

'I can see that,' spluttered the mayor, 'but Marshal Fox can't an' I don't think he would be too bothered either.'

'Then you just go tell the marshal I ain't available right now,' said Brogan. 'When I've finished eatin' I just might consider amblin' up to the saloon or wherever he wants to see me. Right now this excellent stew is far more important than any marshal.'

Mayor Watson could hardly believe his ears and gaped at Brogan for a few moments in total disbelief. 'I ... I can't tell him that!' he eventually exclaimed. 'He's already threatened to have my balls an' I believe him. I ain't about to do somethin' stupid like tell him you ain't comin'.'

'I never said I wasn't goin',' Brogan pointed out. 'All I said was tell him I'm eatin' at the moment an' I just might be along later.'

'Are you mad!' exclaimed the mayor. 'Even if he

doesn't do anything to me, I can't see him taking that kind of talk from you.'

'If you don't tell him you'll never find out will you?' grinned Brogan. 'Now, be a good dog an' run back to your master an' give him the message.'

The mayor threw up his arms in horror, ignoring the reference to the dog and appealed to Maisie. 'Can't you make the man see some sense, Maisie? He's askin' to be measured for a coffin; can't you get through to him!'

'If he wants a coffin, that's his affair,' said Maisie. 'Now do like the man says an' tell the marshal ... oh, but before you do I'd make a detour past your house an' pick up some clean underwear, those you've got on must sure be full now.'

'Mad!' exclaimed the mayor. 'Completely mad! I always knew you were a bit crazy but not as crazy as this. OK, OK, I'll go tell the marshal, but don't try to blame me for what happens.'

'We won't!' assured Brogan. 'Now let me finish eatin'.'

Mayor Watson grumbled out, waving his arms and constantly looking back. His walk back to the saloon was not quite as fast as the walk from it.

On the way Lawyer Green and Councillor Smith joined the mayor and he hastily told them what had happened; both turned to look in total disbelief at Maisie Fullwood's. Very slowly and with a great deal of trepidation, they entered the saloon, resigned to the wrath of Marshal Ebenezer Fox.

The marshal eyed the trio sneeringly and raised

his eyebrows questioningly. The three men looked at each other and Green and Smith slowly took one step backwards, leaving their leader to face the inevitable.

'We ... I ... er ... I found him,' admitted Mayor Watson.

'Well?' asked the marshal, very quietly.

'He ... he says he won't come until he's finished eating,' the mayor gabbled out. 'I did tell him....'

Rather to the mayor's surprise, all the marshal did was laugh. 'I should've guessed as much. I should never've sent someone like you on a man's errand.' He looked at one of the deputies and nodded. 'Where is he?' he demanded.

'In Maisie Fullwood's,' croaked the mayor.

'Where's that?'

'Down the street, first house past the barber's shop.'

The deputy needed no further prompting and, with a completely expressionless face, he stomped from the saloon. Marshal Fox turned his attention back to his glass and, realizing that they were no longer welcome, the three councillors quietly left the room. Once out in the street they walked very quickly to the sheriff's office from where they could see anything that happened in the street.

'Just like I thought,' said Maisie who had been looking out of the window ever since the mayor had left, 'looks like trouble walkin' down the street.'

'A deputy?' asked Brogan, not bothering to look and still eating his stew.

'Biggest of the two,' confirmed Maisie. 'Mean-lookin' bastard, probably never smiled in his entire life. He don't seem in no hurry, but he's headed here all right.'

'He's just makin' sure that we, an' anyone else who happens to be about, sees him,' said Brogan, ripping a piece of bread off a roll and wiping it round his plate. 'That was just about the best stew I ever tasted, Maisie. I'd sure appreciate some more.'

'Sure thing,' said Maisie, taking the plate and going through into the kitchen.

The deputy had reached the window and gazed in, staring unblinkingly at Brogan through the grimy glass. His hand rested threateningly on the handle of his gun and his other hand gently caressed his badge of office. Brogan simply looked up and smiled. Maisie came in, placed the second helping of stew in front of him and she too smiled at the deputy. For a brief moment the otherwise expressionless face assumed a look of pure anger, but it quickly passed and he pushed open the door. Maisie had returned to her kitchen.

'Mr McNally,' said the deputy, very quietly. 'Marshal Fox sent for you. He don't like bein' kept waitin'. When he asks for somebody, they come runnin', no matter what they is doin'.'

'Mr Deputy,' replied Brogan with equal quietness. 'Brogan McNally don't go runnin' nowhere for nobody. If I choose to meet with the marshal it'll be when I'm ready an' not before. Now, you can see I'm in the middle of a most delicious meal an' I intend to finish it before I do anythin' else.'

For the first time the deputy seemed completely at a loss, he simply was not used to anyone refusing. His hand slipped to the handle of his gun and he held it and glared at Brogan for a few moments hoping that he looked menacing enough to frighten the saddle tramp. Brogan turned his attention to the stew, apparently totally unimpressed.

'Hard man!' snarled the deputy. 'Hard man or not, let's see how hard you really are....' His hand moved but before he could draw the gun he froze as something prodded into the back of his head and a woman's voice spoke softly behind him.

'You heard the man, Mr Deputy,' said Maisie. 'He don't want to see the marshal right now, he's eatin' his dinner. I'm sure no decent man would expect anyone to leave perfectly good food.'

The deputy turned his head slightly and saw the barrel of a scatter gun. 'You wouldn't dare fire that thing!' he hissed.

'Just try me!' invited Maisie. 'You wouldn't be the first. I've seen brains splattered across a room before now, messy but it'll clean up OK.'

The deputy thought for a moment and apparently decided, as far as his almost emotionless face would give away, that perhaps he had better not test Maisie's invitation. He released hold of his gun and glared at Brogan.

'Just like a yeller saddlebum, hidin' behind some woman's skirts. You're bein' very stupid, McNally; I can only remember one other feller actin' like you an' refusin' to go to the marshal when ordered. He's feedin' worms somewhere out in the desert now.'

Brogan shrugged. Being called a coward or other insults had very little effect on him although he had long since learned the value of such insults when used upon other people.

'Be a good boy, Mr Deputy,' grinned Brogan, 'leave me to finish my food in peace. You can tell your master ...' – he deliberately chose the word and watched the deputy bridle – 'just what I told the mayor to tell him. Right now I'm eatin' an' maybe, just maybe, all dependin' on how I feel, I might just come along to the saloon, or anywheres else he's a mind to be.'

'I think you just made yourself one very dangerous enemy!' warned the deputy.

'Enemy?' queried Brogan. 'I thought lawmen were supposed to uphold the law. Why should the marshal be any different?'

'I didn't mean the marshal!' snarled the deputy. 'I meant me!'

Brogan slowly looked the deputy up and down and smiled. 'I reckon I'd take my chance with you any day, Mr Deputy!'

The deputy snarled angrily, turned and stomped out, leaving Brogan and Maisie to smile at each other. However, Maisie seemed to have some doubts as to the wisdom of it all.

FOUR

Marshal Ebenezer Fox did not react quite as his deputy had expected. Instead of bursting into one of his rages – he was well known for his rages – he simply slammed his hand on to the counter and roared with laughter. Even Sam, the bartender, who had seen most things, was rather bemused by the marshal's reaction.

'Is that all you're goin' to do, laugh?' asked Sam.

'Just what the hell else am I supposed to do?' said Fox. 'I'll say this for this saddlebum, he's got some guts, either that or he's just plain damned stupid.'

'He's just stupid!' asserted the aggrieved deputy.

'You think so?' grinned the marshal. 'Well I'm sorry to disagree with you, but I don't. I ain't never set eyes on this feller, I ain't never heard of him, but already I know he's a dangerous man.'

'It would've been a different story if that stupid bitch hadn't had the scatter gun stuck in the back of my head!' complained the deputy.

'Would it, Walter, would it?' said Fox, thoughtfully. 'Maybe you'd've been a dead man by now.'

This time it was Sam who laughed. 'I doubt it, Marshal,' he said. 'Somethin' tells me this McNally ain't that stupid. Sure, he maybe could've outdrawn the deputy here, but I don't think he would've shot him. He's too wily to try somethin' as stupid as that; that would've put him on the wrong side of the law an' given you the excuse to gun him down. McNally ain't no youngster an' he says he's been driftin' all his life an' he also reckons he's never fallen foul of the law yet. I can't see him startin' now.'

Ebenezer Fox was thoughtful for a moment. 'Could be you're right,' he finally admitted. 'All that does is confirm to me that he's probably a very dangerous man to cross.'

'I'll go get him again,' offered Walter, the deputy, 'only this time I'll be ready.'

'An' if he still won't come?'

'Then he'll be a dead man!' assured Walter.

The marshal smiled and patted his deputy on the shoulder. 'Forget it, Walter, forget it. You're a good deputy an' I'd hate to lose you. Just mark this one down to experience.'

'There was that other feller who tried somethin' like this back in Salt Springs,' said the other deputy, whose name was Grant. 'He ain't around no more.'

'He was different,' sighed the marshal; 'he was just a young punk who'd had more drink than he could hold. Mark my words, this one is somethin' else.'

'I'd still like to stand against him in a fight,' said Walter.

'Fist or gun?' smiled Fox.

'Either,' said Walter.

'An' you might lose in either,' said Fox. 'OK, we wait for this McNally to come to us. In the meantime I'm hungry an' since the only eatin' place in town is this Maisie Fullwood's, I suggest that you …' – he looked at Sam – 'arrange for her to send some food in here. After Walter's run-in with her I ain't so sure as it would be such a good idea to eat there.'

'No problem,' agreed Sam. He left the saloon by the back door.

'I ain't never seen you act like this before,' said Grant, the other deputy. 'Normally you'd fly off in a rage if anyone dared to question you or refuse somethin' like that.'

'How old are you, Grant?' asked the marshal, with a faint smile.

'Twenty-six,' replied Grant.

'An' you, Walter?'

'Twenty-four – I think,' said Walter.

'Which means I'm older'n your ages added together,' said the marshal. 'That also means that I've had a hell of a lot more experience of the world an' men, especially men like this saddle tramp.' He smiled broadly. 'Oh, yes, I have come across men like him before an' I've got to admit that I've come off worst more times than I've won. Just trust my feelin's about this feller an' don't either of you try nothin' stupid an' definitely don't do anythin' unless I say so.'

'If that's the way you want it,' agreed Walter. Grant also nodded his understanding.

At that moment a small figure, dressed in the sombre black of an undertaker, entered the saloon and walked timidly towards the three lawmen. He raised his hat and gulped slightly.

'Mr Fox, sir, Marshal Fox?' he almost whispered.

'That's me!' grinned the marshal. 'I'd say you was the undertaker in this town.'

'Jeremiah Gibbons,' said the undertaker with due deference.

'What can I do for you, Mr Gibbons?' smiled the marshal. 'I hope you ain't toutin' for business, we ain't ready to die just yet.'

'No ... no,' assured Jeremiah Gibbons. 'It's just that as the undertaker for this county, it is also my duty to store bodies until their internment, unless the relatives have the body at home that is. In the case of the outlaws there are no known relatives, at least not in this county, so I have to keep them. The point is, Marshal, what do I do with them? I was told to do nothing until you had arrived. Mayor Watson did not want to order their burial just in case you had to take the bodies back with you.'

'He's right about that,' said the marshal.

The undertaker gulped and shuffled uneasily, twisting his black top-hat nervously in his hands. 'I ... I feel that I must advise you that already they do not smell very pleasant. In this heat dead flesh decomposes very quickly. It is, of course, entirely your own concern. How far would you need to travel with them?'

'Nelson City,' replied Fox.

'Four days,' said Gibbons. 'I suppose if you don't mind the smell, they will be pretty bad by then.'

Marshal Fox laughed. 'I appreciate your concern, Mr Gibbons, and I take your point. Is there a telegraph office in town?'

'Yes, sir,' said the undertaker. 'As a matter of fact I am also the telegrapher. The machine is in my office. You are most welcome to use it.'

'It's all a matter of identification,' said Fox. 'Normally I am expected to take the bodies into Nelson or some other big town where there's a judge, but it's been three days an' as you say, another four to go. I doubt if any judge would want to try an' identify a rottin' corpse. I'll wire Nelson, confirm the men are who they are, that should be enough.'

'Mayor Watson has already wired Nelson City,' said the undertaker. 'He wanted to know what the procedure was to pay out the reward due on them, so they already know the men are dead.'

This news did not seem to go down too well with Ebenezer Fox and he showed his displeasure in no uncertain terms. He slammed his fist on to the counter and snarled,

'What the hell did he want to do that for? He knew I was comin' here.'

The undertaker seemed almost apologetic. 'I'm sure you're right, Marshal,' he said, sniffing. 'However, that is what he did and it was not for me to question his actions.'

'Damn the man!' muttered Fox. 'I ain't blamin' you, but it just wasn't necessary.'

Jeremiah Gibbons shrugged. 'Anyway, they

know now. Do you still want to use the telegraph?'

'Yeh, I guess so,' growled the marshal. 'I'll be along in a few minutes.'

'As you please,' said the undertaker. 'I'll go and open up the office.' He left the saloon obviously relieved that his ordeal was over.

'What's so important about the mayor tellin' Nelson?' asked Deputy Walter.

Fox sighed and shook his head. 'How long have we been tailin' them three?' he asked. 'I'll tell you how long, almost a month. You know darned well how we gets paid, we gets paid on results, we collect the reward. This means that this saddle-bum, McNally, has already staked his claim an' there ain't no way we can deny him his legal right.'

Grant nodded sagely. 'An' you was hopin' to persuade him that he didn't want the money, or even tell them in Nelson that it was us who killed them, so's we could collect.'

'You got it!' grumbled the marshal. 'A month of hard work has just flown out the window, we get nothin'!'

'All the more reason for lettin' me kill the bastard!' said Walter. 'Just say the word.'

'If only it was as easy as that!' said the marshal. 'If that stupid mayor hadn't let Nelson know, it would've been easy. We could've told McNally that he had to come back with us an' sign a few forms an' things. It could just have been that he might've had an accident on the way an' had they not known in Nelson, they would've been none the wiser.'

'Couldn't he still have an accident?' asked Walter.

'Don't be so stupid!' growled Fox. 'How d'you think it'd look? We've already got enough enemies in high places an' they would seize on any opportunity to discredit us, me in particular. We'd've had a few awkward questions to answer an' we still wouldn't've got our hands on the money.'

'So it looks like we lost out,' said Grant.

Ebenezer Fox remained thoughtful for a few moments and then slowly nodded his head. 'There is one way,' he said eventually. 'We let McNally collect, even help him as much as we can. He collects an' then we collect off him.'

'You mean kill him after he's got the money?' asked Grant.

'I can't see any other way,' said Fox. 'I did the same thing once before, before I met up with you two. As far as I know that man's body was never found. He was a drifter, just like McNally, so nobody bothered to look for him.'

'Sounds good to me!' agreed Walter. Grant, too, nodded.

'Then let's look as if we're doin' the right thing,' said Fox. 'I'll go send a wire to Nelson City an' then we'll tell McNally he's got to come back with us to collect. First though I reckon I'd just better take a look at the bodies. I know damned well it's them, but in this case I'd better do it all by the book. If McNally should decide to come while I'm gone, buy him a drink but don't either of you try anythin'. He's our next meal ticket an' we've got to look after him. Got that?'

'I don't like the thought of bein' nice to that man,' said Walter, 'but if that's the way it's gotta be, then you'll find out just how nice I can be.'

'An' don't let him goad either of you,' warned the marshal. 'If I'm any judge that's just what he'll try to do.'

'We'll be discretion itself!' laughed Grant.

'You don't even know the meanin' of the word!' snarled Fox.

Brogan waited for what he thought was time enough to allow Marshal Ebenezer Fox to work himself up into a good temper before deciding to go to the saloon. Sam had been in and told Maisie to provide three meals but he had not talked to Brogan. Maisie suggested that Brogan should take the three plates to the saloon since he was going there anyway. Brogan agreed, but pointed out that he was not a messenger boy. The remark did not impress Maisie at all.

'Your dinners!' announced Brogan as he entered the saloon. He was not surprised to find that the deputies were the only customers, although he did look about for Marshal Fox. Under normal circumstances the bar would have been quite busy at this time, but the citizens of Spencer had all suddenly decided that they had far more pressing matters to attend to at home.

'Put 'em down over there!' instructed Walter. 'Marshal Fox won't be long, he's wirin' Nelson City to confirm the identity of the outlaws.'

'You ain't takin' 'em back with you then?' said Brogan.

'The undertaker reckons they stink too much,' said Grant; 'that kind of stench we can do without, it looks like we're goin' to have enough with your stink.'

'My stink?' asked Brogan.

'Yeh, that's what he said,' said Walter. 'Marshal Fox'll do all the explainin' when he comes back.'

'He more'n likely thinks he can't trust boys to do men's work,' said Brogan.

'Very funny, McNally!' scowled Walter. 'Think what you like, it don't hurt us none. I'll even buy you a drink just to show I don't hold no grudges.'

'Now that's an offer I can't refuse,' grinned Brogan. 'A beer will do fine.'

Walter nodded at Sam who pulled the beer and waited expectantly for the money. Walter grinned and threw a coin on to the counter.

'It looks like you're goin' to become a rich man,' continued Walter. 'Ten thousand dollars, that ain't bad money. You should be able to retire on that much.'

'I can't say as I've any plans to retire,' said Brogan, making a great show of sipping his beer. 'I can't say as I'll know what the hell to do with money like that either, but I reckon I can have a good time findin' out.'

'By rights that should've been our money,' said Grant. 'We've been tailin' them three for long enough.'

Brogan smiled. 'That's the way it goes sometimes. Some you win an' some you lose. It looks like you just lost this one.'

Walter and Grant exchanged quick glances,

thinking that Brogan had not noticed, but they were quite wrong, Brogan rarely missed even the slightest of things like that. He had seen enough to know that all was not as it seemed. At that moment Marshal Ebenezer Fox stomped back into the saloon.

'At last!' he said, sounding more pleased than Brogan knew he really was. 'The elusive Mr Brogan McNally.'

'Marshal!' acknowledged Brogan. 'Sorry I couldn't get round to seein' you sooner, but I had a meal to eat. Talkin' of eatin', I brought your food from Maisie. If I was you I'd eat it while it was still hot. That's mighty good stew, the best I tasted in many a month. It'd be a pity to let it go cold.'

'He's right!' said Fox, going to the table where the food was. The other two joined him. 'Bring your beer, McNally,' continued the marshal, 'we can talk while we're eatin'.' He indicated a fourth chair. Brogan accepted the invitation.

For a couple of minutes no words passed between them as the three lawmen tackled the stew. It was quite plain that they appreciated what they were eating.

'You were right about one thing, McNally,' announced Grant. 'This is sure some tasty stew.' Brogan nodded and sipped his beer.

'Now, McNally,' said Marshal Fox, wiping his mouth on his sleeve. Brogan did not really like being called McNally, he prefered plain Brogan, but in the case of Marshal Ebenezer Fox he was more than happy to make an exception. 'I've just wired Nelson City to confirm that the men you killed were the outlaws, Jones, Hobday an' Grimaldi. Mayor Watson had wired earlier I believe, informing them at Nelson City of what had happened. There should be no problems from now on. You'll get your money OK.'

'I never doubted it,' said Brogan. 'So what they goin' to do, wire it through here somehow? There ain't no bank in Spencer.'

'That's the problem,' said Fox. 'In the normal way the president of the local bank would have been wired an' he would have been authorized to release the money but, since there is no bank, it means that you will have to go to Nelson City to collect it.'

Brogan nodded. At least that made sense, although he was not too happy at the prospect. He mentally cursed the town of Spencer for being so short-sighted.

'As far as I can remember,' he said, 'I ain't never been to Nelson City. How far?'

'Four days ridin',' said Fox. 'Easy enough goin', mostly scrub an' desert, but there's plenty of water; all you'll need is enough food for four days.'

'That I got,' said Brogan. 'Anyhow, there's plenty of food even in the driest desert if you know where to look. Biggest problem is usually enough water for a horse.'

'Things like lizards, rattlesnakes an' bugs!' sneered Walter. 'Yeh, I heard some folk ain't all that fussy about what they eat.'

'Have you ever eaten rattlesnake or lizard?' asked Brogan.

'Nope, never had to come down that low!' said Walter. 'Have you ever eaten bugs?'

'A couple of times, when there's been nothin' else at all,' admitted Brogan. 'They ain't so bad providin' you just close your eyes an' swallow. At least they keep you goin' a while. In some places some Indians eat 'em all the time.'

'We ain't stinkin' savages!' growled Walter.

'That's what them Indians think about us!' grinned Brogan. 'OK, so it takes four days. I ain't so sure as I'd feel all that safe in your company.'

'Why not!' laughed Fox. 'Sure, I can understand you thinkin' we're sore about you beatin' us to the reward but I don't hold no grudges. Before I was made a marshal I made my livin' bounty huntin' an' sometimes some other bounty hunter'd beat me to the kill, but we didn't hold no grudges against each other; we all knew we'd beat someone else at some other time, so it all worked out even.'

'Maybe so,' said Brogan, 'but I hear you've got somethin' of a reputation about always gettin' your way an' it's a pity on the man who crosses you. Well I reckon I just crossed you.'

'Yeh, I hear I got that reputation too,' laughed the marshal. 'I hear it all the time. I was beginnin' to wonder if there was someone else callin' himself Marshal Ebenezer Fox goin' about pretendin' he was me.'

'An' I think I upset your deputy here as well,' said Brogan, 'leastways he said I'd just made an enemy of him.'

'Take no heed of Walter,' laughed the marshal,

'he's young an' don't take too kindly to old men like you an' me gettin' the better of him. I'm sure he only said that in the heat of the moment. Ain't that right, Walter?'

'Sure,' said Walter, not very convincingly to Brogan's ears. 'I was just a bit sore at bein' taken by surprise like that, especially by a woman.'

'One thing I learned many years ago,' said Brogan, 'was that it don't ever do to take no woman for granted an' it don't do to think they ain't capable of shootin' a man. I'd rather face a man with a gun any day than a woman.'

'Why, 'cos you don't like killin' women?' sneered Walter.

'Nope,' replied Brogan. 'I ain't never had the need to kill me a woman yet, but if I had to I would. No, it ain't that. If a man is goin' to shoot you he'll aim for the chest or the head. A woman don't think like that, she may kill a feller eventually but it's an even bet that the first thing she'll shoot at will be a feller's balls. I seen it happen; it seems to give 'em some sort of satisfaction. Balls first, chest or head later.'

Marshal Fox laughed. 'You never spoke a truer word, McNally; I've come across quite a few men who've been left impotent by some woman. Anyhow, you ain't got nothin' to fear from us. They all know in Nelson City that we're escortin' you back there an' they all know that it's you an' you alone what's got any claim on the reward. If anythin' happens to you we don't get our hands on it.'

'So what happens to it?'

'That all depends,' shrugged Fox. 'Usually the next of kin get to collect.' He laughed again. 'Believe me, if I had any next of kin an' they knew I had that kind of money comin', I'd be more scared of what they'd do than any outlaws or someone with the reputation I seem to have. In your case, since you don't have no next of kin, it's up to the governor what happens to it. Usually he gives small amounts to somethin' like the local orphans, but big amounts like you're entitled to, he may give them some an' keep the rest in State funds.'

'Meanin' his own pocket!' suggested Brogan.

The marshal shrugged and smiled. 'I wouldn't know about things like that. Anyhow, the point is you're safe enough with us; we don't stand to gain one cent by killin' you or if you had an accident. Anyhow, you ain't got that much choice. If you want the money you've got to go to Nelson City to collect it.'

'An' if I don't?'

'Who knows?' grinned the marshal.

FIVE

Brogan had heard enough and seen enough to know that all was not as straightforward as it seemed. Marshal Fox's explanation was perfectly logical; there was no bank in Spencer and it was highly unlikely that any individual could raise that kind of money and even if they could, it was doubtful if they would rely on some official in a distant town to guarantee the outlay.

Sitting in a pile of straw alongside his horse, Brogan mulled over the situation. As was quite usual in such circumstances Brogan resorted to asking questions of his horse.

'Do you think we ought to go to this place Nelson City?' he asked her. She shook her head savagely. 'No? But then you wouldn't, it's four days ridin' an' these days you'd rather spend your time in some stable or other. You're gettin' lazy in your old age.' This time she shook her head and gave him a wide-eyed stare. Brogan laughed. 'Damn it, you're right, what the hell would we do with that much money? Maybe it'd be better if we forgot the whole idea.' This was greeted with an enthusiastic nodding. 'OK, I'll think about it, sleep on it overnight.'

As he had been talking, Brogan's hand had slipped to the handle of his gun. Even as he had talked aloud, his keen hearing had picked up the faintest of sounds, a sound which did not belong in the expected order of things. Casually he stood up and ambled to the stable door, which was slightly ajar. He stood and listened for a moment and then suddenly crouched and swung into the opening, his gun aimed steadily.

'What the hell d'you think you're doin'?' This alarmed question came from a shadowy figure now within about six inches of the barrel of Brogan's gun.

'Matt Fry!' exclaimed Brogan. 'More to the point, what the hell do you think you're doin'? I could've blasted a hole in your skull. Don't you know it just don't do to creep up on a man like that?'

'How the hell did you hear me?' asked a rather frightened Matt Fry. Brogan stood to one side and allowed Matt to enter the stable where the single oil lamp cast a very weak, yellow light. 'I could hardly hear myself.'

'I can hear a fly land on a piece of shit from a hundred yards,' boasted Brogan. 'The question is, just what were you doin' creepin' up on me like that?'

'I heard voices,' explained Matt. 'I couldn't think who you were talkin' to.'

'My horse,' said Brogan.

'Two voices, I heard two voices. Don't tell me that horse of yours can talk.'

'Naw, 'course she can't,' laughed Brogan. 'That was all me, I often talk to myself.' He had also been quick to notice that Matt Fry was once again wearing his sheriff's badge of office. 'I see you decided not to quit after all.'

'They talked me into it,' admitted Matt. 'Mind you, I've got to admit I didn't take all that much persuadin'.'

'Now there's no danger!' jibed Brogan. 'The marshal is headin' back to Nelson City in the mornin', I'm supposed to be goin' with him.'

'That's what I came over to talk to you about,' said Matt. 'I just came to warn you that you're more'n likely headin' straight into a trap. I did hear that some other feller had to go to Nelson to collect a reward. As far as I know he ain't never been seen since.'

'Don't you think I know that,' laughed Brogan. 'Anyhow, if you'd been listenin' to what I said to my horse, you'd know that I ain't so sure about goin'.'

'What about the reward?' said Matt. 'Ten thousand is a lot of money to just pass up on.'

'I've passed up on more'n that,' grinned Brogan. 'You can believe this or believe it not, just as you please, but money just don't mean that much to me. All I need is a few dollars in my pocket to pay my way an' I'm happy.'

Matt Fry smiled and shook his head. 'Now if any other man had made a claim like that, I'd've called him a liar, but you, yeh, I can believe that's just what you think. If you'll take my advice, you'll just ride on out of here an' forget all about the reward an' Marshal Fox.'

Brogan laughed. 'Sheriff, if I got one failin' at all, it's that I can't take advice. If somebody tells me I ought to do somethin', I tend to get a bit difficult an' almost always end up doin' the opposite.'

'If you reckon you don't need the money, why the hell bother?'

'I can't argue with that,' agreed Brogan. 'The only thing is once I get my teeth into somethin' I can't let go. This time I got my teeth into Marshal Ebenezer Fox an' his deputies. I want to make sure that they don't get their stinkin' hands on the money. No, you just made my mind up for me, I'll go to Nelson City, collect the reward an' then I'll more'n likely give it all away. I might even stand in the street an' throw it to the wind an' watch folk scramble for it. At least that way I'll know they can't ever get their hands on it, 'ceptin' maybe what they can catch.'

'You're crazy!' muttered Matt Fry. 'Just one thing. Before I came here, I overheard them two deputies talkin'. It seems one of 'em, I ain't sure which, hates your guts so much he's even ready to kill you before you reach Nelson City. I heard him say since they've got nothin' to lose now, he's goin' to make sure you don't collect either.'

'Just talk,' said Brogan. 'I reckon they've already got it worked out. They allow me to collect an' then they kill me. That's the only way it'd make any sense.'

'An' you're still goin', even knowin' that?'

Brogan laughed. 'We all got to die sometime!'

* * *

Maisie Fullwood provided Brogan with enough food to last about two weeks, let alone four days and she refused to take any payment. All she did was elicit a half-hearted promise from Brogan that he would come back and visit her, although neither of them really believed that he would.

Marshal Ebenezer Fox and his deputies emerged from the saloon about half an hour after the sun had risen, all three looking very dirty and very sour. It became rapidly obvious that all three had learned not to even speak to each other first thing in the morning. It took the marshal all his time to acknowledge the presence of Brogan.

Saddling their horses took the best part of another half-hour, during which time Brogan simply sat and stared at them, all the time smiling. This seemed to annoy them, although none said a word, but they made their feelings very plain. Brogan continued to smile just to see how long it would take for one of them to crack. Deputy Walter proved to be the first to give in.

'What the hell have you got to grin about?' growled Walter. 'That's all you done all mornin', sit there an' grin. Hell, I seen men killed for doin' less than that!'

'I'd say I got ten thousand reasons to smile,' said Brogan, knowing that such a statement was likely to upset the deputy even more.

'Bastard!' muttered Walter.

'True,' said Brogan with an even bigger grin. 'My ma an' pa was never married, leastways not as far as I know. In fact I don't think my ma was all that sure just who my pa was. More'n likely he was a sailor – I was born in Seattle, that much I do know.'

'Where the hell's Seattle?' grumbled Deputy Grant. Marshal Fox had remained stubbornly silent and continued to do so.

'Way up north,' grinned Brogan. 'Right up Canada way.'

'Don't even know where Canada is,' muttered Grant.

'If you ever want to make it to marshal, you gotta know things like that,' goaded Brogan. 'Ain't that right Marshal?'

Marshal Fox grunted something that nobody could quite translate into English and rode off expecting the others to simply follow, which they did. For the moment at least Brogan felt safe enough, he sensed that both deputies were under strict orders.

The trio of councillors, Mayor Watson, Lawyer Green and Councillor Smith were lined up outside the sheriff's office and briefly acknowledged the departing marshal, but when he completely ignored them, they were obviously very annoyed. Brogan gave them a smile as he passed and touched the brim of his hat. This just seemed to add insult to the occasion.

The reappointed Sheriff Matt Fry was not in evidence, although Brogan did catch a glimpse of him at the office window. He was obviously not prepared to meet Marshal Ebenezer Fox even at that late stage. Brogan thought that perhaps the sheriff was well advised on that point.

The first part of their journey was through the
farmlands of Spencer County and took them
about four hours. News of their coming had
somehow sped ahead of them, although to the best
of Brogan's knowledge nobody had left the town of
Spencer before they had. However, it seemed that
they were expected all along the route.

From a brief conversation Deputy Walter had
with one small boy, it seemed that nobody was
interested in the marshal nor his deputies, the
one man everyone wanted to see was the man who
had killed the three outlaws. Both deputies
seemed rather annoyed that the dirty saddle
tramp with them should be the centre of
attraction and not them. To Brogan, the reason
was obvious, killings were virtually unknown in
the county and a killer was almost someone from
the stars.

From odd snippets of conversation Brogan did
overhear, it seemed that most thought he must be
under arrest but they could not quite work out
why he had been allowed to keep his guns. One or
two suggested that it was because the Indians in
the hills had been restless of late. Whatever
people thought, neither Brogan nor the deputies
chose to correct them. Marshal Fox remained
stubbornly silent throughout, simply staring
ahead as if seeing nothing.

They cleared the farmlands just after midday
and were soon into dry scrub which gradually
gave way to open desert. They stopped once

shortly after reaching the edge of the desert at a large, clear waterhole, where, for almost the first time, Marshal Ebenezer Fox seemed to come to life after splashing cold water on his face.

'Another three hours an' we'll call it a day,' said the marshal. 'There's good water an' shelter. I see you finally stopped your grinnin'. I know what you was doin', I know your type, McNally. I know I told Walter an' Grant to hold themselves, but if you keep on like that I ain't goin' to answer for what they do.'

Deputies Walter and Grant were actually some distance away and could not hear what was being said. They seemed deep in conversation between themselves.

'Couldn't resist it,' said Brogan. 'You've been around long enough Marshal, I'd say you an' me was about the same age, although I ain't sure just how old that is. I reckon you must've tried rilin' some youngsters before now.'

The marshal gave a brief and rare smile. 'Sure, I guess so, but I'd watch it with these two; they'll kill you or anyone else just as easy as they'd step on a bug. I gotta admit they scare the hell out of me sometimes. If they hadn't teamed up with me I reckon they'd've been just about the most savage pair of outlaws you could ever see.'

'That's just about the way I had 'em figured,' said Brogan, smiling at the pair as they glanced in his direction. 'OK, you got a deal, Marshal, I won't try to rile 'em again, leastways not until we get to this Nelson City place an' I've collected the money.'

'Very wise,' nodded the marshal. 'Speakin' of money, just what the hell do you intend to do with what you got comin'?'

'Probably I'll give nearly all of it away,' smiled Brogan. 'I did have this idea of standin' in the street and throwin' it all in the air just to watch folk scramble for it.'

Ebenezer Fox plainly did not believe a word of what Brogan was threatening. To him it was inconceivable that a man could have no real interest in money. He smiled, sighed, shook his head and indicated that it was time to move on.

As before, Brogan chose to ride behind the lawmen – purely an instinct of self-preservation – although he did not really expect any problems. This time however, he looked at the trio in a very different light.

There had been something in the way that Marshal Fox had spoken at the waterhole which made Brogan think that perhaps all was not as well as it appeared between the marshal and his deputies. He knew that the warning about Walter and Grant – who turned out to be called Walter Jefferson and Grant Philips – had not been intended as a threat in any way, it seemed to be an almost genuine warning. Brogan began to wonder just how long the unholy alliance between the three would last. He had suspicions that it was destined to break up fairly soon one way or another and, most likely, quite violently. He had his chance to question Walter and Grant when they made camp for the night in the lee of a large, hollowed-out cliff face.

* * *

'Bein' a deputy marshal sure seems one hell of a hard way to make a livin',' said Brogan as he warmed up some hash that Maisie Fullwood had wrapped.

'It ain't so bad,' muttered Grant. 'We gets by all right.'

Both men were close to drooling at the sight of Brogan's hash. Brogan laughed and emptied another wrapped parcel of the delicious smelling mix into the pan.

'I got plenty,' he said; 'it's gotta be eaten anyhow, it won't keep much longer. There's plenty for all of us.' This obviously pleased the deputies and for just about the first time since he had seen them, both men smiled.

Marshal Fox had disappeared behind a rock to attend the natural functions of his body and was out of earshot. Brogan pressed ahead with his questioning, having loosened their attitudes and tongues with the promise of good food. He knew he had to take advantage of the absence of the marshal knowing that they would clam up if he was within hearing.

'All we got is dried pork an' beans,' grunted Walter.

'That'll keep, this won't,' said Brogan. 'I still reckon there must be better ways to earn a livin' than riskin' your lives huntin' outlaws. Pay can't be all that good....' He pretended he did not know how they were paid. 'No more'n ten dollars a week, an' I'd say you'd be lucky to get that.'

'We don't get paid like that!' grunted Walter. 'We takes any reward money.'

'So that's why you're sore at me!' Brogan grinned. 'I just took the bread out of your mouth.'

'Somethin' like that,' muttered Grant.

'So you just lost somethin' over three thousand dollars,' continued Brogan. 'That sure is a lot of money to lose.'

'One thousand apiece,' said Grant. 'We gets one tenth each.'

Brogan was genuinely surprised. 'Only one tenth!' he exclaimed. 'You mean that he stood to get the rest?'

'That's just about the size of it,' sighed Grant.

'Hell, man, you'd be better workin' on your own, you know, bounty huntin' for yourselves.'

'We've thought about it!' snarled Walter.

At that point Marshal Fox returned and Brogan handed him a plate of hash. The marshal took it as casually as if he had been expecting it and had every right to it. There was no word of thanks or praise, not that Brogan wanted any. Later he brought up the question of the reward with the marshal.

'They was mutterin' on about my doin' 'em out of the biggest pay day they ever had,' said Brogan, nodding at the two deputies some distance away.

'The biggest pay day I would've had too,' said the marshal. 'Still, that's how it goes sometimes.'

'A thousand apiece though,' continued Brogan, 'that don't seem all that much. They reckon they only get one tenth of any reward money.'

'They should learn to keep their big mouths

shut,' grumbled Fox. 'What they don't tell you is that I pay all expenses, everythin' includin' food, bullets, clothes an' shoein' of horses. What they get is theirs to keep, do what the hell they want with. Sometimes I have to hand out a few bribes to make folk talk. They don't pay for things like that, I do.'

'Maybe it's fair maybe it ain't,' shrugged Brogan. 'I just thought I'd better tell you I got the impression they wasn't too happy with the arrangement. If I was in your position I'd be watchin' my back when they were around.'

The marshal laughed loudly, making the deputies look up but they seemed to ignore him as he continued to laugh. Eventually he stopped and in a whisper to Brogan said, 'Don't you think I do that all the time already?'

'Then why stick with 'em?' asked Brogan.

'That's easy!' said the marshal, quietly. 'I ain't gettin' no younger. There was a time when I could race about like a jack-rabbit, but not now. I need them to do most of the leg work. Not only that, they're very fast an' very accurate with both hand guns an' rifles an' possibly most important of all, they ain't afraid to kill nobody at a nod from me.'

'Maybe you'll nod once too often an' they'll shoot you,' suggested Brogan.

'Nothin' more certain one day, if I keep 'em on long enough. I was thinkin' of lettin' 'em go their own way after this job.'

'You could recommend 'em for marshal.'

Once again Ebenezer Fox broke out into laughter and once again the deputies looked up.

Deputy Grant even suggested that they share the joke but the marshal simply waved them away and they returned to their own deep conversation.

'Sure, I could recommend somethin' like that,' he replied when he had stopped laughing. 'McNally, I got this badge 'cos I was a thorn in the side of authority. Things was gettin' so bad that the only thing they could think of was to make sure I was on their side. In their wisdom they decided to make me a marshal an' I accepted on my terms. I accepted 'cos it gave me some sort of respectability and authority. This badge gave me powers the likes of you could only dream about....'

'It made your murderin' all legal!' said Brogan.

'You got it!' agreed the marshal. 'There's a good many in high places who'd be only too pleased to see some outlaw blow my head off an' there's even more who would like to see them two suddenly disappear from the scene. How wouldn't matter. The point is they've got about as much chance of bein' made full marshal as I have of growin' wings an' flyin'. As things stand at the moment their jobs depend on me stayin' alive. If I go, they know darned well that they go too.'

'So if they kill you they lose their jobs? I wouldn't rely on that state of affairs too long. As I see it they can see ten thousand dollars disappearin'. When was the last time that kind of money was put their way?'

'Never,' replied Fox. 'The most has been two thousand up to now. Mostly it's been a lot less than that, but we've always made enough to get by pretty well.'

'Ten thousand is one hell of a lot of money,' said Brogan. 'Leastways as far as men like that are concerned. It could be that it might be just too much for 'em to resist.'

'Don't you think I ain't considered that already,' smiled Fox. 'Right now though, I'd say it was you what had the problem, not me. It's you who's collectin' so it's you who's goin' to be the target for them an' probably a few others in Nelson City. Then there's at least two other bounty hunters based on Nelson as I know too an' believe me, bounty hunters ain't no different to nobody else, they'll kill a man like you just as easy as they would an outlaw an' they'll hide your body somewhere knowin' darned well that there ain't nobody goin' to bother lookin' for you.'

'You included?'

'Me included!' admitted the marshal with a wide grin.

Brogan laughed lightly. 'I know I allus said I can trust a man who's honest, but in this case maybe your honesty means I'd better watch my back with greater care than usual.'

Marshal Ebenezer Fox simply laughed and announced that he was turning in for the night. Shortly after that the deputies also pulled their blankets across them. Brogan stared into the fire for about another half-hour before he decided that he was safe enough for the moment and that it was time to sleep.

SIX

Brogan had an untroubled sleep, although he had over the many years he had been wandering, developed the technique of both sleeping and being able to hear every sound around him. There had only been one sound which was alien to the normal sounds of the night and Brogan had briefly held his gun at the ready. In the event it turned out to be nothing more than Deputy Grant Philips having to relieve himself.

As he had expected, Brogan discovered that he was the first to waken, the opening of his eyes coinciding almost instantaneously with the first hint of dawn. He did think about waking the others but decided that his breakfast, provided by Maisie, was not going to be shared. Breakfast, actually quite a rarity for Brogan, consisted of a piece of cold meat pie. The one thing that Maisie had forgotten was coffee, although he did have some in his saddle-bag but he decided to wait and see if the lawmen were going to make coffee.

Almost an hour later the three men awoke, coughed and spat and appeared to be in thoroughly bad tempers and, apart from briefly splashing water on their faces and hissing painfully as the cold water they drank coursed through rotten teeth, there was no other attempt at breakfast or coffee.

Once again saddling their horses seemed to take a long time, but eventually they were following Marshal Fox along the dusty trail in a general westerly direction, which put the glare of the sun behind them, for which Brogan was quite pleased. Once again he rode in the rear and this seemed to be accepted and it was not until they stopped at about midday beside a small waterhole that anyone really spoke to each other.

This pattern was repeated for the next two days and they arrived in Nelson City shortly before sunset on the fourth day.

'You'll have to wait until tomorrow morning!' announced the judge to whom Marshal Fox had reported. 'There's no banks open at the moment and I don't intend ordering one to open just for you.' He sniffed the air in the confines of his office and looked hard at both men facing him. 'It seems to me that both of you could do with a bath. See to it that you have one before I see you in the morning.'

Marshal Fox smiled and glanced at Brogan but Brogan always seemed to take any suggestions about baths or soap and hot water very personally. He simply glared defiance at the judge.

'Bathin' ain't healthy!' Brogan declared when they were outside. 'I had me an all-over wash against my will once, some nuns down in Mexico. I caught a cold for the first time in my life an' it almost killed me.'

'Don't you ever bath?' laughed Fox.

'Sometimes; last time was about six months ago, I give myself an all-over soak in some pool or other, but I sure don't strip off or anythin' like that. Mind, there was once I did have a proper bath, you know hot water, soap an' me stripped off sittin' in the tub, but I was covered in mud an' the woman I was stayin' with insisted.'

'Did you catch cold that time?'

'No, can't say as I did,' said Brogan, 'but I reckon that was more good luck than anythin' else.'

'Well all I can say is you'd better have a bath before we see the judge again tomorrow,' advised the marshal. 'Judge Collins don't take kindly to folk ignorin' his instructions.'

'He can go to hell!' asserted Brogan. 'I ain't on trial for nothin' so what I do or don't do ain't no concern of his.'

Fox laughed. 'I reckon you'll tell him so too!'

'Why not?' nodded Brogan. 'He can't do nothin' about it.'

'Maybe not,' grinned the marshal. 'Anyhow, there ain't nothin' we can do until tomorrow. There's a doss house near the stable you left your horse. Hotels in this town are mighty particular about who they take. Most folk like you end up in one of the doss houses, we got two of 'em. There ain't nothin' to choose between either.'

'I already made my arrangements,' said Brogan.

'Feller at the stables agreed I could sleep alongside my horse.'

Fox gave a sardonic laugh. 'Why not? Some horses ain't that fussy who they bed down with. Anyhow, I got things to do; you'll just have to look after yourself. You just be here at ten in the mornin', preferably smellin' a lot sweeter than you do now, but that's your affair.'

'I'll be here,' assured Brogan.

Marshal Fox walked off down the street and Brogan looked about at the seemingly endless mass of people. Nelson was a big town and, apart from a brief visit to Phoenix, the biggest town he had ever been in.

They had ridden in down the main street, a wide street lined with what seemed like countless stores, saloons, gaming-houses and at least two whorehouses. Apart from the possibility of a glass of beer, the attractions of Nelson had little appeal for Brogan. In fact he felt an overpowering urge to take his horse and ride out there and then. He disliked towns and cities. His instinct was to get the hell out of it just as soon as he had collected the reward in the morning.

The reward! He wandered slowly along the wide boardwalk thinking about what he was going to do. He finally came to the conclusion that he must have been mad to agree to come to Nelson. He did not really want the money, although he would keep perhaps a couple of hundred for himself. What he was going to do with the remainder he simply had no idea.

Brogan soon discovered that there were at least

six other streets off the main street, each almost as busy, although there were rather more hotels and lodging-houses. He stopped and looked in the windows of various saloons and a couple of hotels, trying to make up his mind if he would venture inside and sample the beer. The hotels he discarded, not because he was afraid of being evicted, but because such apparent luxury was completely alien to him. The saloons seemed to offer the best solution.

Quite deliberately he chose a saloon which appeared to be rather more rundown than the others, masquerading under the name of the Black Diamond. His first impression about it seemed proved correct as it was far more the type of place to be found in most of the smaller towns. Sawdust carpeted the floor and the occupants were quite plainly either fellow travellers or possibly the less desirable elements of Nelson City society.

The bartender simply looked at him and raised an eyebrow and Brogan ordered a beer. There were a few casual and largely uninterested glances in his direction and a well-worn bar-girl sidled up to him and gave him a broad, decayed-tooth smile from beneath caked-on make-up and invited him to share the delights her body had to offer. Brogan decided that he found the large Maisie Fullwood far more attractive and politely but firmly refused. The girl simply shrugged and turned her attentions to another customer.

'Seen you ride in with that bastard Fox,' said

the bartender quite unexpectedly. 'I heard there was someone comin' to collect a reward. All I can say is good luck to you, anyone who does that bastard out of any money is a friend of mine.'

Brogan smiled and sipped at his beer, which he found to be very good. 'If you know that, I reckon the whole town must know,' he observed.

'Most,' agreed the bartender. 'It's only happened once before as far as I can remember an' I heard rumour that that feller didn't live too long afterwards. Nobody ever bothered about it though.'

'Most folk just don't want to get involved in somethin' that ain't their business,' said Brogan. 'Big town you have here, only place I seen bigger is Phoenix. I don't like towns, I can't wait to get out of here.'

'I'd watch your back,' advised the bartender. 'There ain't just Fox an' his deputies, there's a good many others who'd skin a turd for a dollar, so what they'd do for what you got comin' is anyone's guess.'

'So I hear,' said Brogan. 'I seen some nuns in the main street. I wouldn't've thought this would've been the sort of place for folk like that.'

'The Poor Sisters,' grunted the bartender. 'Good folk; if it wasn't for them there'd be dozens of kids roamin' loose on the street. They run the orphanage, been here a good many years. I was an orphan kid myself, I reckon it was only them what kept me out of a whole load of trouble.'

'Orphanage!' mused Brogan. 'Now there's an idea.'

The bartender looked quizzically at him but said nothing. Brogan drained his glass and left the saloon, aware of a few watchful eyes. By that time it had grown quite dark and the saloons, hotels, gaming-houses and whorehouses were all lit up in preparation for the evening trade. Brogan wandered back to the main street and began looking.

About ten minutes later he found what he was looking for, the figure of a nun bustling along the boardwalk carrying two heavy bags. He quickly drew alongside her, raised his battered hat and smiled.

'Heavy bags you got there ma'am,' he said. 'Here, let me carry 'em.'

The nun looked at him strangely but raised no objection as the stranger took the bags. 'Why thank you, sir,' she said, smiling weakly. 'I can manage though, I do it most days.'

'No trouble ma'am,' grinned Brogan.

'Sister!' corrected the nun. 'Not ma'am, just Sister.'

'If you say so,' agreed Brogan. 'How far you got to go?'

'About half a mile, just on the edge of town,' replied the nun. 'What do you want, Mr … er….'

'McNally, ma'am … I mean Sister,' said Brogan. 'Brogan McNally. I don't go much on the McNally bit, you can just call me Brogan.'

'Well, Brogan,' smiled the nun, 'I may be a nun but I am not entirely naive of the ways of the world and men. In my experience there are very few men – or women – who carry heavy bags for the likes of us purely out of the goodness of their heart. What can I do for you, Brogan?'

'I never was very subtle,' said Brogan. 'OK, Sister, you got me weighed up. All I wanted to know was where the orphanage was an' I figured that was where you was goin'.'

'Correct!' agreed the nun. 'Why should a man like you, who is quite plainly a man who is used to wandering and not, I venture to say, of religious inclination at all, why should you want to know where the orphange was?'

'Right on both counts,' laughed Brogan. 'I ain't no city man, that's a fact an' I ain't been inside no church – leastways not to pray – in my life. It's like this, I got me this problem an' I'm lookin' for someone to help me out.'

'I would suggest that someone like Father Grey would be more suitable. The Sisters Of The Poor are not really the best people to help out with personal problems.'

Brogan laughed. 'That's just where you're wrong, Sister. This time I reckon you're just the folk I need.'

The nun looked at him strangely and then laughed. 'If you say so. However, I am definitely not the person you need to speak to. I am simply one of the sisters. Mother Beatrice is the one you need to see and she does not have a very high regard for men.'

'Includin' this Father Grey?'

'Including Father Grey!' nodded the nun. She pointed to a large house just visible at the far end of the street. 'That's the orphanage. I'll introduce you to Mother Beatrice, and may the Good Lord help you.'

'It ain't the Lord who's goin' to do any helpin',' said Brogan. 'That's what I want to talk about.'

'Intriguing!' laughed the sister, but she did not ask any further questions.

'Mr McNally!' A very deep voice boomed out of a rather small and fragile-looking body as Mother Beatrice entered the small room where Brogan had been ushered. 'I am very busy and I do not normally talk to strangers, but Sister Mary seemed quite insistent. If I did not know her better I would say you have made quite an impression upon her.'

'Most folk reckon the biggest impression I make on 'em is the way I smell,' laughed Brogan.

Mother Beatrice sniffed and nodded. 'That too,' she agreed. 'Now, Mr McNally, what is it that only I can help you with?'

Brogan was about to suggest that she use his first name, but decided against it. 'Well, it's like this, ma'am....' He was uncertain of exactly how to address her but she raised no objection to being called "ma'am". 'Maybe you've heard about me, it seems most folk in Nelson City have … I rode in with Marshal Ebenezer Fox this afternoon....'

'The Devil's right-hand man!' snorted Mother Beatrice.

'I'll not argue with that,' said Brogan. 'The point is I'm due to collect a big reward for killin' three outlaws....'

'Yes, we have heard,' said the nun, 'but we did

not know who it was and it is really unimportant as far as we are concerned.'

'Is somethin' like ten thousand dollars unimportant?'

Mother Beatrice managed a faint smile. 'Since the likelihood of us ever coming into that kind of money is too remote to consider, then it is completely unimportant.'

'So how would you like ten thousand, less say a couple of hundred?'

Mother Beatrice stared at Brogan for a few moments as she digested the possibility. 'Mr McNally,' she eventually whispered, 'I'm sure I must have misheard you. Are you offering me ... this orphanage ... almost ten thousand dollars?'

'That's just about the size of it!' grinned Brogan.

She looked completely at a loss which, Brogan correctly guessed, was something new to her. 'Please, Mr McNally, if this is some kind of sick joke, I must ask you leave this instant.'

'It ain't no joke, ma'am,' assured Brogan. 'Maybe I'd better explain.'

'I wish you would, Mr McNally,' she said, sitting on a nearby chair and indicating that he sat on the chair opposite.

'Well, ma'am, it's like this. I been wanderin' all my life, it's been my own choice, that's the way I like it. In all that time I ain't never had the need for much money, just so long as I have enough to get by an' pay my way. I ain't never murdered nobody; I ain't never stole nothin' off nobody an' I ain't never assaulted any woman....'

'I find that difficult to believe of any man!' she

snorted.

'I ain't sayin' as I've never killed a man,' said Brogan; 'I must've done to be collectin' this reward an' there have been others, possibly too many, but it was always in self-defence or defendin' someone else. Now you can believe that or not, I don't much care. The point is I got money comin' to me an' I just don't want it, so I got to thinkin' what the hell I was goin' to do with it an' then I found out about the orphanage.'

'I must beg your pardon if I seem sceptical, Mr McNally,' said Mother Beatrice, 'but in my experience, and believe me my experience is quite considerable, nobody, but nobody, gives that kind of money away, even to a good cause like this orphanage, without demanding or expecting something in return. What do you want of us, Mr McNally?

'Well for a start you can quit callin' me Mr McNally,' grinned Brogan. 'The name's Brogan an' I'd be mighty pleased if'n you was to use it.'

'That's not what I meant, Mr McNally!'

'I know what you mean about folk usually wantin' somethin' in return,' said Brogan, 'but this time I don't want a darned thing. All you gotta do, to make it all legal like, is be at Judge Collins' office at ten in the mornin' an' have it all signed over proper.'

'It all sounds too easy, Mr McNally, much too easy. I am not a young woman and I admit to having been on this earth for a little over seventy years. In all that time the one thing I have discovered is that nothing ever comes too easily.

I'm sorry if I seem disbelieving, but I still cannot believe that any man, and more especially a man like you, would simply give away that much money.'

'A man like me?' laughed Brogan.

'I mean no disrespect, Mr McNally,' smiled the nun, 'but I suspect that your interest in religion is almost nil and certainly at the very bottom of any priorities you may have. You are quite obviously a travelling man, a drifter with no ties either of family or even emotion. I suspect that death means very little to you, even your own. Oh, I have no doubts about your assertions that you have never committed any crimes, at least crimes against the civil code but whether your claims of self-defence or even the defence of others would satisfy a Christian moral code is very question-able. That you rarely bath or wash is quite apparent, although not at all unusual and of little importance, but all this does not in any way reconcile with you offering to donate such a large amount of money to our cause.'

'I think you lost me somewhere in all that,' smiled Brogan. 'Don't you want the money?'

Mother Beatrice smiled. 'Of course we do, we are not a wealthy organization, although we get by. The money would solve quite a few problems we have.'

'Then quit arguin' an preachin',' said Brogan. 'The money's there just for the takin', so thank God, or whatever you do, an' be at the judge's office in the mornin'.'

Mother Beatrice studied Brogan for quite a long

time before replying then she suddenly laughed. 'Why not? We certainly have nothing to lose. Even if this turns out to be some form of sick joke we lose nothing since we never had it. Very well … Brogan, I shall be there; I only hope you will be there as well.'

'This ain't no joke,' assured Brogan. 'I guess you just about got me right when you said I ain't got no interest in religion. I like kids though an' they need folk like you to look after 'em while they're young. I only wish there'd been somethin' like you when I was a youngster, maybe things would've turned out different, who knows?'

'Do you want things to be different?'

Brogan laughed. 'Naw, not now, it's too late for me; I'm past savin' an' certainly past settlin' down. Some day someone's goin' to get the better of me an' shoot me an' that'll be that. There sure ain't nobody to shed any tears over me.'

'It is never too late to change,' said Mother Beatrice.

'Then that's where you an' me have to disagree,' laughed Brogan. 'I couldn't imagine nothin' more borin' than livin' in the same house in the same old town for the rest of my life. If you don't mind, I'll stay as I am.'

'The Good Lord gave man freedom to choose,' she smiled. 'How you exercise that right is up to you. Very well, Brogan, I shall meet you in Judge Collins' office at ten o'clock in the morning. Until then may God keep you safe.'

Brogan laughed and patted the Colt at his hip. 'I'd rather rely on this than God.'

'Unfortunately, so would the majority,' she sighed. 'Now, you must excuse me, I have work to do.' With that Mother Beatrice left the room and shortly afterwards another nun came to show him to the door.

Satisfied that he was doing the right thing, Brogan slowly ambled back to the Black Diamond where he ordered another beer. It was quite obvious that he had acquired a certain notoriety as all conversation and card playing ceased the moment he entered. He could feel greedy eyes boring into his back and could almost hear the thoughts of a large number of the customers.

Thoughts of where, when and how to relieve this dirty saddle tramp of his money seemed to occupy many. Although he did not know it, another strong rumour had also circulated, the rumour that here was the fastest man with a gun anyone had ever seen. Brogan was enlightened on this point when the bartender served him his beer.

'You're a marked man,' he said, quietly. 'I ain't done this much trade in twelve months. Word got round that you was here earlier an' there's nothin' like a gunfighter to attract all the scum an' a few young bucks who fancy their chances.'

'Gunfighter?' asked Brogan.

'That's the name you got,' confirmed the bartender. 'It came on ahead of you. How true it is I don't know an' care even less. Most is thinkin' about takin' your money, but there's a couple who I think just want to test how good you are.'

'Where?' asked Brogan, not turning but looking

in the large mirror behind the counter in which he could see almost the whole room and its occupants.

'Just behind the door,' replied the bartender. 'They can't be much more'n eighteen or nineteen.'

Brogan could just see the young men in question but not too clearly. Casually he turned, glass in hand and pretended to survey the room. The two young men were staring at him, sneering and toying with empty glasses. Suddenly one of them stood up and walked purposefully towards the counter. The other followed a few paces behind.

'Hi there, old man!' grinned the leading youth. 'We hear you come into some money, a lot of money. I think it'd be a mighty neighbourly gesture if you was to buy everyone in this room a drink; it ain't often we gets a real celebrity in here.'

Brogan's casual manner did not outwardly alter, but he was steeled ready to move. He deliberately looked the youth slowly up and down from head to toe, knowing that it may well annoy him. He was right, the youth did seem to take exception.

'Are you sure you're old enough to be drinkin' boy?' Brogan grinned eventually.

'At least I can take it!' growled the youth. 'Which is probably more'n an old man like you can.'

'OK, boy,' said Brogan, 'say your piece or make your play, I'm tired an' I want my sleep, us old folk need our sleep. It seems you got somethin' to prove, so try an' prove it.'

'That kinda talk can get you killed!' warned the other youth, standing alongside his friend. Suddenly there was a lot of noise as customers of the Black Diamond in the likely line of fire scuttled to the edges of the room.

'Just like I thought,' said Brogan. 'You is all talk!'

Both youths moved at the same time but they stopped in mid-draw and stared in horror down the barrel of Brogan's Colt. Brogan laughed, reached forward and took their guns out of their hands and threw them on the counter.

'Bang, you're dead!' laughed Brogan. 'If I was you I'd scuttle back home an' tell your mothers your pants need changin' an' tell her to dry behind your ears.'

The youths looked at each other and gulped. 'Yes, sir,' said one, eventually. 'We didn't mean nothin' really. I guess we'd just had too much to drink.'

'Then take your guns an' get on out of here,' advised Brogan.

The youths grabbed their guns and ran out, turning to mutter some dark threats as they left. Almost immediately the room was a babble of voices, everyone now convinced that this saddle tramp was indeed the fastest man with a gun anyone had ever seen. Even the bartender seemed suitably impressed.

'Your standin' an' reputation just went up a whole lot of notches,' he said, 'an' I don't reckon that's a good thing. All it'll do is make a whole lot of others try an' outdraw you.'

'After tomorrow I won't be around,' said Brogan. 'They'll soon forget all about me.'

'Maybe it ain't a bad thing that you do keep movin',' said the bartender. 'That way you ain't a sittin' target.'

'I guess that's one reason,' admitted Brogan.

However, whatever the effect upon the remaining occupants of the saloon, Brogan sensed that the two youths he had just made look very small would not be quite so impressed. He somehow knew that he would be meeting them again in the not too distant future.

SEVEN

Shortly after the youths had left and the furore had subsided somewhat, two other figures entered the saloon. The effect upon a large number of customers was to make them drink up, fold up hands of cards and decide that it was about time they were in bed. The two men strolled over to Brogan.

'We heard you've just put on somethin' of a show,' said Deputy Marshal Grant Philips.

'News travels fast,' sighed Brogan. 'I hope you two ain't of the same mind.'

'Naw, we know better,' grinned Deputy Walter Jefferson. 'We just happened to be passin' when we heard what happened so we thought as how we'd just make certain it was you.'

'So you found out,' replied Brogan. 'As far as I know I ain't broken no laws.'

'We never said you had,' said Walter. 'It would've served them two right if you'd killed 'em. Couple of young tearaways. So far they ain't done nothin' they can be arrested for, but it's only a matter of time.'

'So what can I do for you?' asked Brogan.

'Nothin', nothin' at all,' assured Grant. 'So tomorrow you'll be a rich man. You could've bought us a drink with the money, but the pity is we won't be around. We have to leave town.'

'I don't suppose many folk will lose much sleep over that,' smiled Brogan, 'not if the way you cleared this place out as soon as you came in is anythin' to go by.'

'Most of 'em got cause to worry,' said Grant.

'So you an' the marshal is leavin',' said Brogan. 'I was supposed to meet him in Judge Collins's office.'

'Won't make any difference to that,' said Walter, 'all that's just a formality. You've gotta be there though or else you don't collect.'

'I'll be there!' assured Brogan.

'An' then what,' asked Grant, 'back to Spencer?'

'Spencer! What the hell would I want to go back there for?'

'I dunno,' shrugged Grant. 'I just sorta figured since you was there you might've been goin' somewheres that took you through there.'

'Chance, that was all took me to Spencer,' said Brogan. 'I've been travellin' all my life, goin' somewhere an' nowhere. Maybe I am headin' some place, I don't know. The only thing I do know is if I am, I ain't reached it yet.'

'So where you goin' next?' asked Walter.

'Wherever takes my fancy,' replied Brogan. 'All I do is point my old horse an' see where we ends up.'

'Well it's desert east an' south,' said Grant, 'but then you know that I reckon. Due west is high mountains. North is the easiest way.'

'I like an easy life,' grinned Brogan, knowing

that the two were simply intent on finding which way he was going. 'Maybe I will head north. I'll have to think about that.'

'That's one hell of a lot of money to be carryin',' said Walter, 'an' there's more'n one of the rats that ran out of here when we came in as would be only too ready to relieve you of such a heavy load.'

'An' they know I know it!' grinned Brogan. 'Naw, I don't reckon as I've got that much to worry about with any of 'em; it's all wishful thinkin' on their part. I got a feelin' that them two boys might be a bit different though; they ain't interested in the money, leastways it ain't their prime interest. I made 'em look the punks they is an' I get the feelin' they don't like that. No, if there's any trouble goin' to come my way it'll be from them, or maybe from you.' He looked meaningfully at Walter.

Walter laughed a little uneasily. 'On account of what happened an' what I said back in Spencer?' Brogan nodded. 'Naw, don't worry none about that. I was mighty sore at the time I gotta admit, but that's all over an' done with now.'

Brogan did not believe the deputy for one moment but did not say so. 'So what takes you out of town in such a hurry?' he asked.

Deputy Grant produced two Wanted posters and showed them to Brogan. 'Four thousand dollars, that's what,' he said. 'We got news they're close by. They was sighted back west towards the mountains.'

'The best of luck,' smiled Brogan. 'I guess that means this is the last we'll see of each other. I can't say as I'm sorry about that, that'd be tellin' lies an' I don't tell lies too often.'

'The feelin's mutual,' assured Walter. 'Anyhow, we're for turnin' in right now, we got an early start in the mornin'.'

Brogan smiled to himself as they left, now completely convinced that he might very well have Marshal Ebenezer Fox, Deputy Grant Philips and Deputy Walter Jefferson to deal with as well as two young tearaways. Even the assurances of the bartender who, like all good bartenders, had overheard every word, did not make him think otherwise.

'I saw them posters,' said the bartender; 'it's true, they was seen due west in the mountains an' headin' this way.'

'Maybe so,' nodded Brogan, 'maybe so!' Then, for the sake of any messages getting back to the marshal, which he felt was a distinct possibility, he added, 'They is headin' west, me, I'm headin' south, desert or no desert. I don't mind, I've learned how to survive for weeks in a desert.'

'If you say so,' said the bartender with seeming uninterest. 'Me, I'd take the easy way an' as the man said, that's due north.'

'You ain't me!' asserted Brogan with a grin, reasonably sure that the information would soon reach the marshal.

Brogan had expected some form of trouble from the two youths, whom he had discovered were brothers, Pete and Al Steiner, but in the event this concern, what little there was, proved unfounded. He spent an undisturbed night in the stable and was up and about just before dawn, just in time to witness three shadowy figures on horseback quietly leaving town in their usual early morning moods.

He watched the trio of lawmen head west, although he suspected that they were deliberately making something of a show of heading in that direction. Nevertheless, the trail to the west was the one they took.

He breakfasted on some more of Maisie Fullwood's food and decided that it was now past its best, although he had eaten far worse and did not waste any of it. He spent the next hours until it was time to be at Judge Collins's office simply sitting outside the stable watching Nelson City slowly come to life.

As in most towns, the first to appear were the store owners, although he did note that they were about an hour later than they would have been in a smaller town. Gradually more people began to appear, most obviously going off to some place of work. From where he was he could see a large sawmill which seemed to employ most of the townsfolk. There was another, smaller building which also seemed to employ quite a few people, but he never discovered what they did and was not all that interested.

Ten o'clock found Brogan standing outside the office of Judge Jacob Collins, but the judge himself did not make an appearance for another twenty minutes. He made no apology for keeping Brogan waiting, eyeing him with obvious distaste and sniffing the air.

Brogan had expected Mother Beatrice from the orphanage to be on time and he was beginning to wonder if she had decided against coming, but she showed up a couple of minutes after the judge. She smiled at Brogan, who had been left in a small outer office and made some comment about knowing that the judge was never on time and that she had had other matters to attend to.

The judge seemed in no hurry to get the business over and done with but he did stop and stare at the nun during one of his frequent, noisy, passages between his office and another office.

'Mother Beatrice,' he said, 'do you have an appointment?'

'I believe so,' replied the elderly nun. 'I was asked to be here by Mr McNally.'

'McNally?' queried the judge, raising his eyebrows and glaring at Brogan.

'Sure, I asked her to come,' confirmed Brogan, 'on account of I'm givin' most of the reward to the orphanage.'

'I beg your pardon?' exclaimed the judge.

'I'm givin' almost all the money to the orphanage,' repeated Brogan. 'I don't need it an' they do. There ain't nothin' wrong in that, is there?'

Judge Collins was plainly taken aback. 'No … no, I don't suppose there is.' He looked hard at Brogan again. 'Most unusual!' he muttered. 'Indeed, most unusual!' He shook his head and was about to return to his own office when Brogan spoke.

'What's the hold up, Your Honour?' It went

against the grain slightly to address the judge in this way, but he felt that discretion was in order.

'Mr Evans, the president of the bank,' muttered the judge, 'he's late and there is no point in proceeding until he comes, he's bringing the money with him.'

'Don't nobody keep to time in this town?' grunted Brogan.

The judge smiled briefly, which was apparently a very rare occurrence. 'I wouldn't have thought that time was very important to a man like you, McNally.'

'Normally it ain't,' admitted Brogan, 'but I hate hangin' about. I could've been on my way by now. I'm sure you don't want the likes of me hangin' about in your nice clean town.'

'Too true, McNally, too true,' replied the judge. 'Don't worry, Mr Evans will be along very soon and then you can be on your way.' As he spoke the outer door opened and a portly, very well-dressed man entered, carrying a briefcase. 'Ah, speak of the devil, here he is now. You have the money Mr Evans?'

'All here,' confirmed the bank president, looking questioningly at Mother Beatrice.

'Then let us get matters over and done with,' said the judge, 'the quicker the better. Please come into my office, Mr Evans, Mother, McNally.'

'Mother Beatrice?' queried Evans.

'Yes,' the judge said slowly. 'It would appear that Mr McNally is something of a philanthropist despite his appearance and unsavoury body odours. He says he is donating the reward to the orphanage.'

Evans looked a little bewildered but said nothing as he followed the judge into his office followed by Mother Beatrice and Brogan. The judge indicated a chair for the nun but left Brogan to stand. Evans took up a position at the side of the large desk and opened the briefcase, producing several documents which he handed to the judge.

'Have you done this sort of thing before, McNally?' asked the judge, glancing through the papers.

'Killed outlaws?' queried Brogan.

'No, had to sign for rewards,' said the judge. 'I have little doubt that you have killed before, many times I would say, and not only outlaws.'

'A couple of times,' said Brogan. 'Never nothin' as formal as this though. It's only been with the local sheriff or mayor an' someone from the bank.'

'We do things rather differently in Nelson City,' said the judge with a rather condescending air. 'We are rather better organized than some towns. Now, there are three documents to be signed. You do know what I mean by documents do you not?' Brogan nodded and sighed wishing he would get on with it. 'Good, it makes things so much easier. All that is required is your signature at the bottom of each.' He looked up over the spectacles he was wearing and smiled sardonically. 'Of course if you can't write you will simply make your mark and it will be witnessed. Since Mother Beatrice is here she will make an ideal witness.'

'I can read an' write,' growled Brogan, who

always took offence at the suggestion that he might not be able to.

'You can?' said the bank president. 'Most unusual. I have only ever met one saddle tramp before who could read and write.'

'Then I guess you ain't met that many saddle tramps!' muttered Brogan.

'Thankfully, very few,' admitted Evans.

'Then sign here,' said Judge Collins, handing one of the documents to Brogan and indicating a pen and an inkwell.

'I said I could read as well,' grinned Brogan, deliberately studying the paper, mainly to annoy the judge and the bank president.

'I have no doubt that you can,' sighed Judge Collins, 'but I can assure you, Mr McNally that you have nothing to fear. All these documents are for is to make the handing over of the money legal.'

Brogan smiled and decided that he really did not have any reason to doubt the judge and reached for the pen. He signed with something of a flourish and, after examining the signature and grunting, he was handed the other two which he again signed.

'Thank you, Mr McNally,' said Evans, opening the briefcase again, taking out several bundles of money and placing them in front of Brogan. 'Count it if you wish, but there is no need, it is all there.'

'I believe you,' grinned Brogan, picking up the nearest bundle and extracting several notes, which he counted. 'Three hundred, that'll do me fine.' He pocketed the money and waved his hand to Mother Beatrice. 'The rest is all yours.'

For the first time, the elderly nun showed some emotion as she took a bundle and fingered it with great reverence. 'I ... I honestly believed this was some sort of joke, Mr McNally. I'm still not convinced that it isn't or that I am not dreaming.'

'It's no dream,' laughed Brogan. 'Hell, I must be plain loco. All that money an' all I can do is give it all away.'

The judge 'Mmmphed' and shuffled a little uneasily in his chair. 'I wish you had let me know about this, McNally,' he said. 'I could have arranged for the necessary document of transfer to be drawn up.'

'I don't need none of your legal documents,' grinned Brogan. 'All I done is give my own money to Mother Beatrice here. Since when did that need a piece of paper signin'?'

The judge looked up at the banker who was toying with the clip on the briefcase., 'I ... er ... I agree, it's your money to do just what you want with, but it is most unusual.'

'Do you usually get saddlebums givin' their money away?'

Evans looked rather uncomfortable and shook his head. 'I must confess that I have never had such a thing happen to me before, nor have I ever heard of it happening.'

'Then you got somethin' to tell your grandchildren!' laughed Brogan. 'Now, if that's all there is to it, I reckon it's just about time I took my stinkin' body out of Nelson City.' He moved to the door and looked back at the still unbelieving Mother Beatrice. 'You just make sure nobody else don't get their hands on that money, Sister,' he said.

Mother Beatrice managed a weak smile. 'I can assure you that all this will be used diligently and for a good cause ... Brogan. I really don't know how to thank you, I wish there were some way.'

'No thanks needed,' smiled Brogan. 'You just make sure you get that lot safely deposited in the bank. I reckon there's quite a few in this town, big an' clean as it might be, as'd have no problems with their conscience if they was to relieve you of that much money.'

'Quite so,' agreed the banker. 'Mother Beatrice, perhaps you will allow me to escort you to the bank where we can ensure that it is credited to the account of the orphanage.'

'It just goes to show what a bit of money can do,' smiled Mother Beatrice. 'A few weeks ago I was asking about the possibility of a loan and you did not seem interested. I wonder if you would refuse that loan now?'

The banker blushed and busied himself in returning the money to his briefcase. 'We can discuss that further if you wish,' he mumbled. Mother Beatrice just laughed and stood up.

'They say money ain't everythin',' said Brogan, 'but it sure opens a lot of doors.'

Mother Beatrice smiled and suddenly went up to Brogan and stood on tip-toes to give him a kiss on the cheek. If Brogan's weather-worn features could ever be said to blush, they did so at that moment.

'Thank you!' said Mother Beatrice. 'Wherever you go, whatever you do, may God go with you.'

'I'm a loner!' Brogan grinned weakly. 'Even He don't go some of the places I go.'

The nun looked at him for a moment and then turned to the banker. 'Shall we go then, Mr Evans? I do have other work that requires my attention.'

Brogan stood aside as Mr Evans and Mother Beatrice brushed past and out into the street. The judge coughed to attract Brogan's attention.

'I must confess to being completely bemused by your actions, Mr McNally,' he said. 'I have never before met anyone who appears to have such a disregard for money. I readily admit that I have very little time for your type, but in your case I must say that I am happily proved wrong. I do not pretend to know or understand either you or your reasoning but what you have done is very noble, very noble indeed.'

'There ain't nothin' noble about it,' laughed Brogan. 'I just don't need the money, that's all there is to it an' I reckon they need it more'n most.'

The judge shook his head and pretended to be busy with the documents Brogan had signed. Brogan took the hint and left.

He was just in time to see Mother Beatrice precede the banker through the doors of the bank and then he wandered back to the stables where he saddled his horse and informed her that they were once again on the move. She did not seem too impressed with the idea.

*   *   *

Having told the bartender that he intended heading south across the desert, information which he was quite certain had found its way back to Marshal Ebenezer Fox, Brogan did ride out south, but after less than a mile he turned up into an old riverbed and then slowly circled Nelson City until he was heading North.

This deception was not for the benefit of the bartender at the Black Diamond, but for the benefit of anyone else who might just have an interest in him or the money they probably believed he was carrying. As far as he knew nobody else in Nelson City knew that he had donated the reward to the orphanage.

As usual, the day was hot and dry and again, as usual, he was in no hurry, content to let his old horse amble along at her own pace. This northern trail took him through prosperous looking farmland and then through thick forest, which was the apparent reason for the timber mill.

On his circumnavigation of the town, he had crossed a railroad, although he had not heard any trains during his stay. He did notice a siding down to the sawmill, which explained why it was so big. Timber was obviously a big export from Nelson City.

Whilst he had been riding through the farmlands, Brogan had felt reasonably safe. He doubted if even the most desperate of any likely pursuers would dare to take him so close to any farms or houses. However, once the trail was enclosed on both sides by trees, his senses were on the alert.

At first he passed a couple of clearings where a few men were busy trimming the branches of felled trees but these were soon lost and he was very much on his own. The forest seemed to become denser, the trees higher and the trail much steeper.

Three hours out from Nelson City and so far, apart from the few loggers, he had neither seen, heard nor had any sign that there was anyone else in the whole world but suddenly his body tensed, his hearing blocked out all the normal sounds and strained to listen for the unusual. At the same time his eyes searched amongst the trees to his right.

A sudden flight of birds through the treetops about a hundred yards to his right and behind him told him all that he needed to know, that he was no longer alone. He knew that birds did not normally take flight en masse when disturbed by the animals of the forest. In his experience the presence of man was the main cause of a sudden bird flight.

He did not stop, quietly urging his horse forward and from her actions he knew that she too sensed the presence of others. Brogan and his old horse had been together for so long that they had developed a mutual understanding and seemed to know each other's thoughts. He had never given her a name, he had never seen the need to.

'You sense it too?' he whispered to her. 'Yeh, we got company old girl an' I don't reckon it's friendly company either. Why else would they be ridin' through the trees an' not along the trail?'

The horse snorted slightly and nodded her head but did not quicken her pace at all. For another twenty minutes they slowly made their way along the trail until they suddenly came upon a fast flowing stream. Brogan decided that this was as good a place as any to force a showdown with whoever was behind him. He dismounted, knelt beside the stream and scooped up a mouthful of water, all the time scanning the forest for any signs. Again the sudden flight of startled birds told him that whoever it was was not too far away,

'He's sittin' beside that stream!' hissed Pete Steiner to his brother, Al. 'Got the bastard, even a blind man'd have difficulty missin' him from here.'

'You sure about this?' whispered Al. 'Maybe we ought to forget the whole thing. It don't matter none any more; it's obvious he don't intend goin' back to Nelson City.'

'I heard somethin' you didn't, Little Brother,' teased Pete Steiner with a knowing grin. 'How does five thousand apiece grab you?'

'The reward?' said Al. 'Sure I know all about that, it was common talk all over town.' Pete seemed disappointed, he had always assumed his little brother, Al, to be something of a simpleton. 'Only thing is, I don't think he's got the money no more.'

'Now you is talkin' stupid again!' hissed Pete. 'If he ain't got it, who the hell has? Don't talk daft, 'course he's got it.'

'I ain't too sure,' said Al. 'I know folks reckon I'm gone in the head a bit an' maybe it suits me to let 'em think so. I see things that way, get to hear things too. They don't bother none when I'm around 'cos they think I can't understand, but that's just where they're wrong.'

'An' what you seen this time?' sighed Pete.

Al shrugged. 'Maybe it's somethin', maybe it's nothin', but I seen Mother Beatrice from the orphanage payin' in an awful lot of money an' I heard her mention this saddlebum by name.'

'An' what does that prove?' sneered Pete. 'It don't prove nothin', that's what. Can you honestly see any man just givin' that much money to some stupid orphanage?'

'Just sayin' what I seen an' heard,' replied Al.

'Then there's one sure-fire way to find out!' snorted Pete. 'We'll never get a better chance than this....' He raised his rifle, took aim and fired....

The figure crouching by the stream moved strangely for a moment as the bullet slammed into it and then fell to the ground. Pete Steiner was suddenly running from cover, whooping his delight, his brother Al close behind but not quite so noisy about it. They swooped on to the prostrate figure....

EIGHT

'Nice try!' said a soft voice from behind Pete and Al Steiner. 'But you just fell for one of the oldest tricks in the book.'

The youths swung round, Pete with his rifle pointing up in the air and Al, who had drawn his gun as they had dashed forward, aimed somewhere in the general direction of the voice. Neither had a chance to shoot as two shots rang out and they both fell to the ground, screaming in agony.

'It could've been worse!' grinned Brogan, stepping forward to kick both rifle and ancient Adams to one side. 'You could easily be dead.'

Brogan had in fact, shot both of them in the knee, shattering kneecap and joint. Both now clutched at their injuries and rolled round in agony.

'Bastard!' Pete Steiner managed to yell in between his own cries of pain.

'I'll not argue with that,' smiled Brogan. 'You've got a lot to learn, my friends.' He picked up his jacket and briefly examined the hole made by Pete's shot. 'At least you can shoot straight. If that'd been me inside this I reckon I'd probably be dead now.'

Brogan had acted quickly after kneeling beside the stream. He had propped his jacket up with two pieces of wood and had placed his hat on top of it and then hidden behind a nearby bush.

This rather unpalatable fact became obvious to the two youths as Brogan retrieved his battered hat, but at that precise moment they were far more concerned with their shattered knees.

The initial agony had passed and they now nursed their injuries, making occasional grimaces and wincing as they tried to move. Eventually it was Al Steiner who spoke, more to his brother than Brogan.

'I said we should forget it!' he groaned. 'Didn't I just say that? But no, you wouldn't listen would you? Nobody ever listens to Al Steiner, he stupid they all say. Well who's lookin' stupid now, Big Brother?'

Big Brother simply winced and scowled at his younger brother before glaring at Brogan.

'How the hell did you know we was there?' he growled. 'We didn't make no sounds, I made sure of that.'

'You made enough noise to wake the dead!' laughed Brogan. 'Maybe in a few years you'll learn somethin' about trackin' an' bushcraft; maybe, but I doubt it.'

'You ain't gonna kill us then?' asked Al with obvious relief.

'I could an' I don't think there'd be too many folk back in Nelson City who'd lose too much sleep over it,' laughed Brogan. 'I ain't like that though; I don't kill unarmed men – well not usually I suppose. Naw, I reckon you just learned a good lesson, that you ain't no good at trailin' a man. Don't go thinkin' I'm a lousy shot either, believe me, I aimed for your knees an' it ain't often I miss what I aim for, from any distance.'

'What you goin' to do with us then?' grated Pete.

'Do with you?' said Brogan, seeming quite surprised at the question. 'What the hell should I do with you? I'm headin' north an' I can't see either of you bein' no trouble again. I don't know where your horses are, but I'd say they wasn't too far away. You'll make it back to Nelson eventually.'

'It's a damned good job you is runnin' yeller!' hissed Pete, defiantly. 'I gotta warn you, McNally or whatever your name is, you ever show your face in Nelson City again, or if we just happen to come across you, you is a dead man!'

'Callin' me yeller don't hurt me none!' laughed Brogan. 'If ever I do pass through Nelson again – which is most unlikely – I'll be only too happy to shoot off your other knees!'

'He's all talk!' growled Al, referring to his brother. 'Allus has been. I'll tell you now, Big Brother, there ain't nobody gonna take any notice of a cripple!'

Pete Steiner grunted something and held his hand against the injured knee. Brogan laughed again, took the hand gun from Pete's holster and took it and the other two guns to place them on a rock some twenty yards away.

'I'll even leave you your guns,' Brogan smiled as he then mounted his horse. 'If I was you I'd get me to a doctor just as quick as you can. Wounds like that have a habit of turnin' bad an' you might even lose your leg.'

A volley of verbal abuse followed Brogan as he departed, all of it from the mouth of Pete Steiner.

The remainder of that day passed quickly and peacefully enough and Brogan made camp alongside another small stream in which he caught two reasonable sized trout. It was not often that he had the opportunity to eat fresh-caught fish and he had to admit that he was not normally all that keen, but it made a change and it seemed a pity to use his own rations before he needed to. He had considered hunting deer, but decided it was not worth the effort.

Having dealt with the Steiner brothers, Brogan wondered if anyone else from Nelson had had similar ideas but bearing this in mind, he had listened and watched all the time he had been travelling and had not heard or seen anything which indicated in any way the likely presence of anyone. However, that did not mean that Brogan was at all complacent and even as he sat by the fire eating his fish his senses were on constant alert.

Forests were naturally full of sounds which to the untrained ear could have been almost anything, but Brogan, conditioned by the years, had learned to automatically slot each sound into a category and he was right more often than he was wrong. On this occasion all the sounds were easily identified and there was nothing unusual to prevent him from having a night of untroubled sleep.

The following morning however, it was an entirely different matter. Brogan had been travelling for about an hour when he came upon the signpost, a signpost which indicated that Nelson City was only fifteen miles back in the direction he had come. There was a choice of trails, one heading south-west to a place called Brandon, one heading more or less due east to 'Silver Mines, 20 miles' and he wondered if this was the name of a town or some actual mines. He never did discover which.

Since Brandon seemed an indeterminate distance, he decided to keep on heading north which, according to the sign, eventually led to Culver City and was another seventy miles. He had not been surprised that he was still in such close proximity to Nelson City; he certainly had not hurried himself and it had been getting on for midday when he had left. The episode with the Steiner brothers had not taken up all that much time, he estimated perhaps twenty minutes, but it did seem a long time since had had departed. It was at that moment that the first hint of possible trouble came.

It had been a single shot, quite some distance away and he had pinpointed it as coming from the trail which went towards Brandon. At first he thought that it was more than likely to be nothing more than someone out hunting, possibly from

Nelson City or more likely some nearby home-steader. He dismissed the incident and continued his way towards Culver City, although he had little intention of actually going there.

Three hours later found Brogan resting his horse alongside one of the numerous streams which fell rapidly down the ever steepening sides of the valley he was now travelling along and later he had to confess to himself that either he had not heard the signs or he had misinterpreted them. However, for whatever reason, Brogan certainly did not hear and he hardly felt the bullet....

It was dark. At least that was how things appeared to Brogan and he lay for some time gathering his thoughts and quietly assessing the situation.

That he was lying close to a fire seemed quite obvious by the fact that one side of him was almost burning whilst his other side was very cold. He had finally decided that it was dark and that apart from a rather sore head, he was otherwise unhurt. He slowly turned his head and looked about and saw a large shape near his feet close to the fire. Automatically his hand slithered to his gun holster but he knew before he reached it that it was empty. The shape grunted and stood to stare down at him.

'About time too!' boomed the voice. 'I was beginnin' to think you was never goin' to come round.'

'Fox!' exclaimed Brogan, sitting up sharply and regretting his action almost immediately.

'At your service once again, McNally, Marshal Ebenezer Fox,' laughed the voice. 'Mind you, I must be gettin' a lousy shot in my old age, you should've been dead now.'

'That was you?' asked Brogan, somehow not at all surprised. He held his head for a moment. 'I should've guessed. I always was suspicious, you seemed to take it too easy. I knew you'd make some sort of play to get your hands on the money. I had hoped you'd've got the message an' headed south.'

Marshal Fox laughed. 'Almost had us fooled too!'

Brogan looked about but could see no sign of the two deputies. 'Us?' he queried.

'Well, me,' admitted Fox. 'Sure, we was told you intended headin' south, through the desert an' at first we all fell for it. But then I got to thinkin', wonderin' just what the hell I'd do if I was in your position an' I finally decided that I'd probably let it drop out, casual like, to some bigmouth that I was headin' in one direction when I was really headin' some other.'

'So what happened to your deputies?'

Fox laughed loudly. 'They thought they knew best; they thought it'd be perfectly logical to lose yourself out in the desert, so that's where they headed. They made it plain that when they did catch up with you they were takin' all the money for themselves.'

'OK,' said Brogan, 'I get the picture but I reckon you must be pretty sore at not findin' any money on me.'

'Three hundred an' forty-two dollars, sixty-three cents,' said Fox. 'I've got another confession to make, the only reason you're still alive is because I want to know just what the hell happened to the rest of it.'

Brogan sat down by the fire and reached for a coffee pot standing on a flat stone close to the flames. The marshal tossed him a tin mug and Brogan poured the coffee. 'I reckon you never believed me before but you gotta believe me now. I seem to remember sayin' somethin' to you about givin' it away, well, that's just what I did.'

Marshal Fox sighed and threw some more wood on to the fire. 'I sorta guessed that's what you'd done an' I gotta admit that I never believed you'd really do it. All I can say is you must be completely loco. You just gave it away? I'll bet you didn't just stand in the street like you said you might an' throw it in the air.'

'I seriously thought about it,' said Brogan. 'Naw, I decided that was a stupid idea, so I gave it all, 'ceptin' three hundred, to the orphanage.'

Marshal Fox grunted and prodded at the flames of the fire. 'I still can't understand you but I guess it serves me right; I should've stuck around an' made sure.'

'Sorry about that,' grinned Brogan. 'It's strange how folk never believe I ain't got no use for that kind of money, but that's the way it is. Now, unless you intend killin' me, I'd sure appreciate the return of my three hundred an' forty-two dollars, you can keep the odd cents.'

'You can go shit for it!' laughed Fox. 'I reckon I

deserve somethin' for all my trouble. Anyhow, I ain't decided if I'm going to kill you or not yet, I'll sleep on it, an' don't think you'll be able to get the better of me, I'm goin' to truss you up like a chicken.'

Brogan shrugged, he would not have expected less. 'There's just one thing puzzlin' me,' he said, 'how the hell did you get so close to me? I allus say there ain't nobody gets that close; I reckon I can hear a man breathin' at a hundred paces.'

'You've been wanderin' all your life, you picked up a few things an' you're probably right, normally a man would never get within shootin' distance. But, you gotta remember, I've been wanderin' all my life too. In fact I reckon if we was to compare experiences we'd find we was almost identical twins, so to speak. Like you I learned my bushcraft an' trackin' skills the hard way. As a matter of fact, I was expectin' trouble from you but I was surprised just how easy it was to get close.'

'Never heard a thing!' grinned Brogan. 'I've got to hand it to you, you're good, the best I've come across yet, 'ceptin' a few Indians. I knew I should've taken more notice of that rifle shot when I was at the crossroads.'

'You heard that?' grunted Fox. 'Yeh, that was me. Saw this rabbit an' just decided he'd make a good dinner.'

'Did you get him?'

The marshal laughed. 'Naw, but he's got a mighty sore ass; I shot his tail off.'

'So what happens now, between you an' them

two deputies of yours? It don't sound like you parted too friendly.'

'They're finished as far as I'm concerned,' replied the marshal. 'They know it too. Unless they can persuade someone into givin' them a marshal's badge or some other marshal takin' 'em on as deputies, I reckon that's one pair I'll be huntin' for the price on their heads before long.'

'Probably,' agreed Brogan. 'How long do you reckon they'll keep lookin' in the desert?'

Marshal Fox shrugged. 'Three, maybe four days. I can't see 'em goin' much longer. Walter Jefferson is a damned good tracker, better'n I ever admitted he was. If he don't pick up a trail in the first two days I reckon he'll put two an' two together an' get the right answer.'

'Then what?'

Again Fox shrugged. 'Probably ride like hell in this direction.'

'What about this outlaw what was seen up near the mountains, won't they go after him?'

'Ain't no point,' laughed Fox. 'He's probably locked away by now, Smoky Johnstone – he's one of the regular bounty hunters – got to him long afore we did. That didn't please Walter an' Grant too much either, but there ain't nothin' they can do about it.'

'You an' them ain't been doin' too good lately. First you lose out to me to the tune of ten thousand dollars an' now another bounty hunter has beaten you to four thousand. The small change you just took off me sure don't stand comparison.'

'That's the way it goes sometimes,' shrugged Fox. 'If it hadn't been for that stupid idea of yours to give it away, I'd be ten thousand the richer now.'

'Yeh!' grinned Brogan. 'I guess that's the way it goes.'

'OK, McNally,' said the marshal, 'it's time to turn in. I'm goin' to tie you up pretty damned tight. Don't try no funny stuff, just remember I got the gun an' I ain't afraid to use it. The only chance you've got of stayin' alive is to do exactly what I say.'

'It seems I ain't got all that much choice,' smiled Brogan, placing his arms behind his back and offering himself to the marshal to be trussed up.

Marshal Fox had kept the fire burning all night, for which Brogan had been most grateful. Unable to move very much, the cold seemed that much worse. He had tried to free himself, but he had to admit that the marshal knew how to tie a man very effectively. The marshal did not seem too bothered about leaving Brogan tied up for quite some time while he prepared some coffee. Eventually however, Brogan was released and spent quite a few minutes rubbing the circulation back into his body.

'Now what?' Brogan asked after about ten minutes of rubbing.

Marshal Fox smiled and prodded some life into the dying fire. 'Now what?' He nodded his head. 'I been thinkin'. First I thought I'd better kill you then I got to thinkin' that why the hell should I?

You ain't such a bad guy, very strange an' unusual but that don't make you a bad guy. In fact I kinda like you. If I do decide to let you go I hope to hell I don't ever see your stinkin' body again, I don't like you that much.'

'An' you're still takin' my money?'

Ebenezer Fox laughed and patted his jacket pocket. 'That's where it is, that's where it stays, until such time as I choose to spend it.'

'You'd leave a man with no money at all?'

'I could take your gun an' rifle too,' said the marshal, 'but I won't, that would be somethin' real mean. No, you can keep your guns but I keep the cash.'

'Thanks for that much anyhow,' said Brogan.

'Don't mention it!' sneered Fox, looking hard at Brogan. 'You heard it too?'

'I heard somethin',' agreed Brogan. 'Not too far away either.'

'Two horses I'd say,' said the marshal. 'To me two horses spells out the names of Jefferson an' Philips.'

'Could be!' agreed Brogan as he reached for the coffee pot and poured some of the hot, black liquid into a mug. 'What's your next move?'

'You got any ideas?' smiled the marshal.

'One,' said Brogan, 'this....'

The scalding coffee flew into the marshal's face and he staggered backwards clasping his hands to his face. Before he had time to do anything else, Brogan's fist had slammed into Fox's stomach followed almost immediately as the man dropped his hands, by another hard blow to the face.

Marshal Fox staggered and fell, blood streaming from his nose.

Brogan leapt forward but the marshal was still very agile and his foot caught Brogan in the stomach as he tried to throw himself at the marshal. Brogan crashed to the ground and suddenly found the marshal on top of him, clawing at his hair and sending a fierce blow straight to Brogan's jaw. It hurt like hell and the marshal was just about to crash his fist into Brogan's face again when Brogan's searching hands found what they were looking for.

The marshal's fist stopped in mid strike as he heard the click of a gun being cocked and he stared into the barrel of his own Colt held firmly in Brogan's hand. He smiled thinly, nodded his head in acknowledgement that he was beaten and started to ease his weight off Brogan's body.

Both men heard the shot but only Marshal Ebenezer Fox felt the bullet. The marshal's body crashed heavily down on to Brogan who chose to lie perfectly still, using the marshal as a shield. His senses had automatically placed the source of the rifle shot – Brogan could tell the difference between rifle fire and hand-gun fire – and he could just make out a figure standing at the edge of some trees some thirty or so yards away. Another figure appeared behind him and the pair stood and looked at the scene below them for quite some time.

Brogan smiled and mentally acknowledged the sense of the two deputies. They appeared to know that Brogan was lying underneath the marshal and that he had a gun. They knew that to rush forward would probably end in one of them and possibly both of them, being shot by Brogan. Wisely they chose to wait.

This impasse continued for quite some time. Brogan estimated at least ten minutes during which time it became quite obvious that Marshal Ebenezer Fox was not dead. Brogan felt him attempt to move and clamped him with his free arm.

'You just stay right where you are!' he commanded. 'Them two think you're dead so if you wanna stay alive, you just play dead. You move one muscle an' they is just liable to make certain that the next bullet is in your brain.' The marshal whispered that he understood and lay perfectly still. 'They gotta make a move sometime,' continued Brogan. 'Right now there ain't much I can do, so we just wait.' Once again Marshal Fox grunted his understanding.

Brogan must have looked away, for the next time he looked for Deputy Marshals Jefferson and Philips, they had disappeared. This rather annoyed Brogan, annoyed him because he had not seen where they had gone. He cursed himself for being so lax and then he simply listened....

NINE

'What the hell's happenin'?' muttered Ebenezer Fox as he continued to pretend death on top of Brogan. 'I can't keep this up much longer, I think I'm hurt pretty bad an' I don't reckon I'll have to play dead much longer. I will be.'

'They've moved,' whispered Brogan. 'I can't see where they've gone, but I reckon they're still watchin'.' He managed to move his head so that he could see to the other side. 'There they is!' he announced. 'Now, if I move fast enough I can get to the cover of that big rock. Where's my rifle?'

'Under my bedroll,' moaned the marshal, quite plainly getting worse. 'What the hell happens to me when you move?'

'You just keep on playin' dead!' instructed Brogan. 'Here, take this.' He thrust the gun into the marshal's hand. 'When I push you off, make sure you lie face down an' keep it out of sight. Reckon you can still use it if you have to?'

'You'd better believe it!' grunted Fox. 'OK, I'm ready when you are.'

'Go!' hissed Brogan, heaving the almost dead weight of the marshal off him.

As instructed, Fox rolled over and lay face down, clutching the gun in his groin. At the same time Brogan first of all rolled into a shallow hollow, grabbed at the rifle under the marshal's bedroll and was suddenly up on his feet in a crouching run for the rock. A series of shots followed his action and he heard a moan and a croaked 'Shit!' from the marshal. Brogan knew that he had been shot yet again.

'Where this time?' he whispered from the safety of the rock.

'Bloody leg!' hissed Fox. 'Thanks for nothin'.'

'Could've been worse,' whispered Brogan.

Brogan cautiously peered over the rock, saw a brief movement amongst the trees and fired. It was obvious that he had not hit anything or anyone, but it did have the effect of making whoever it was scuttle for better cover. For a time there was no movement from the deputies and then a voice suddenly called out.

'You ain't got a chance, McNally!' Brogan recognized the voice as being that of Walter Jefferson. 'How's Fox?'

'Dead!' declared Brogan. 'I guess you just put yourselves on the wrong side of the law.'

'Serves the bastard right!' came the response. 'He tried to cheat us out of that reward money.'

'Just like you said you was goin' to take it all for yourselves!' retorted Brogan.

'He told you that?' came the voice of Grant Philips. 'Yeh, he would say somethin' like that. The truth was that he sent us on some wild goose chase while he came after you. We didn't go far though, we had it all figured out an' we was proved right when we saw them two punks with their knees shot to pieces.'

'Well I got news for you,' called Brogan. 'You, Fox an' them two, you've all been wastin' your time. You all expected to take ten thousand dollars off me but I ain't got it, I gave it all away.'

There was derisive laughter from the deputies. 'You don't expect us to believe that do you? Gave it away! You must think we was born yesterday. We'll make a deal with you, McNally, you hand over the cash an' we'll let you go.'

'And how do you explain the marshal?' asked Brogan.

'There you have another problem,' laughed Jefferson. 'We say that you killed him, that'd sound feasible enough. You'd be a free man, at least you'd be able to get well away, but you'd almost certainly have a price on your head.'

'Which'd give you the ideal excuse to come after me!' laughed Brogan. 'I got news for you: I ain't never had the law on my tail in my life an' I ain't about to start now.'

There was silence for a few moments and then Grant Philips spoke. 'OK, point taken. The deal is you can take old Ebenezer's body with you an' dispose of him when an' where you think fit. The chances are that he'll never be found. We ride back to Nelson an' say we lost the marshal somewhere while we was lookin' for someone else. That way nobody knows anythin'.'

Brogan laughed. 'Fine, that'd be a great idea but there's just one problem, I ain't got the money!

I don't care if you believe me or not, it just happens to be true.'

'So what you done with it?' demanded Walter Jefferson.

'There's one orphanage in Nelson City what is now almost ten thousand better off than it was a couple of days ago!'

'That we don't believe!' laughed Jefferson.

Ebenezer Fox's voice croaked, unheard by either of the deputies. 'Try an' get 'em to come over here!'

Brogan nodded slightly. 'If'n I could trust you, you'd be more'n welcome to come an' search me, you won't find nothin'.'

The deputies appeared to be talking between themselves for a while. 'OK, McNally,' came the eventual response. 'Walter's comin' over. I'm stayin' here to keep you covered. We decided that since you're so damned keen on stayin' on the right side of the law, you ain't about to do anythin' stupid like kill a deputy. You just stand up where you can been seen.'

'I ain't that stupid either!' laughed Brogan. 'I stay here. You come out from those trees where I can see you, maybe then I'll show myself. Just so long as I can see you an' your rifle.'

There was another brief pause while they discussed this. After a time two figures slowly emerged from the cover of the trees. There were a few moments' hesitation before Walter Jefferson started to walk slowly towards Brogan. When Walter was about half way, Brogan slowly stood up, rifle lowered but ready, watching the waiting

Grant Philips for any sudden and unacceptable movement.

Walter Jefferson reached the body of the marshal, stopped for a moment to gaze down at it and seemed to grunt with satisfaction at the sight of the bloodstained jacket. He stepped over the body and advanced upon Brogan....

There was just one shot from the gun in Marshal Ebenezer Fox's hand but there were two shots from Brogan's rifle taken very quickly and unfortunately appearing to miss the intended target of Deputy Marshal Grant Philips. Walter Jefferson made a brief gurgling noise as he collapsed on to the ground but there was no return fire from Grant Philips.

Brogan moved very quickly, dragging the injured Ebenezer Fox, crying out in pain, to the shelter of the rock where he crouched and waited. He had been very surprised when there was no shooting but he remained on the alert for at least twenty minutes, looking and listening. Towards the end of that time he detected the sound of a horse being ridden away and then he relaxed.

'You OK?' he asked Fox.

'Oh, sure,' grimaced the marshal, 'I do this sort of thing every day. My chest hurts like hell, I think that other bullet broke my leg but apart from that I'm fine. I reckon if I don't get me to a doctor pretty damned quick you're goin' to have another corpse on your hands an' a hell of a lot of explainin' to do.'

'I could just leave you,' said Brogan.

'An' if I know Grant Philips he'll arrange for a warrant to have you arrested,' Fox pointed out. 'You need me alive to save your own skin.'

Brogan nodded in agreement. There was logic in what the marshal had said. He sighed and turned over Walter Jefferson's body and confirmed that he was dead.

'I'll go find his horse,' he said. 'It can't be all that far away. Philips has made a run for it, I'm sure of that.' Without giving Fox the chance to reply, Brogan marched off into the forest.

He returned about ten minutes later leading a horse and strapped the deputy's body across it. Ebenezer Fox was in obvious pain and needed help in straddling his horse but before Brogan helped him up, he searched through the marshal's pockets and found a wad of money. He extracted the three hundred and forty-two dollars that was his and stuffed the remainder back into the marshal's pocket without counting it.

'Just takin' what's rightfully mine,' explained Brogan. 'You can keep the odd change.'

Fox grimaced and nodded and Brogan helped him up into the saddle. Five minutes later they were heading slowly back in the direction of Nelson City, Brogan leading the other two horses.

'I hope we make it,' groaned Fox. 'Keep a sharp eye and ear open for Philips. It could be that he's headed straight back, but I doubt it. I reckon he's not far away waitin' to see what happens.'

'Nothin' more certain,' agreed Brogan adding, more to himself than to the marshal, 'How the hell did I get myself in this position? I must be stupid.'

'You an' me both!' grimaced Fox. 'I should've known somethin' like this would happen. I've met types like you before an' almost always come off second best.'

'A very underestimated breed us saddlebums!' grinned Brogan.

Two hours later found them studying the entrance to a small canyon. Brogan had passed through it the previous day and he knew that if anyone wanted to ambush them then this was the perfect spot. While not being very long, perhaps half a mile as he remembered, the sides were sheer, smooth rock, rising some thirty or forty feet. A well-positioned man about half-way could take out a troop of cavalry quite easily.

'You know this area better'n I do,' said Brogan. 'Is there any other way round?'

'Not from here,' replied Fox. 'There is a way back a couple of miles but you almost need to be a mountain goat to get up it. There's a couple of places where you have to get off an' walk.'

'Reckon you can do it?'

'Not a chance!' grunted Fox. 'On your own you could, but there ain't no way I could, not in this condition.'

'An' to go through there could be committin' suicide,' said Brogan. 'Are you ready to do that?'

'If I don't get to a doctor pretty soon I might just as well shoot myself,' said Fox. 'It could be that he ain't up there.'

'Do you really believe that?' grinned Brogan.

'I said could be,' said the marshal. 'I'll stake

everything I own that he's up there just waitin'.'

'So it looks like we got two choices,' said Brogan. 'We can take the chance an' ride through or we flush him out somehow.'

'You ever tried flushin' a rat out?' asked Fox. 'Almost impossible, the rat always finds some crack to hide in.'

'I've flushed out one or two,' said Brogan. 'I reckon you have as well, but this time it looks like I'm on my own.'

'Looks like it,' said the marshal. 'I only wish I could help; it'd give me great pleasure to kill that bastard.'

'You just make sure you don't die on me,' grinned Brogan. 'We'll go down by the river. You'll be safe enough over by that big rock but keep your gun handy just in case.'

The marshal patted his holster. 'I'm ready!' he smiled weakly

Brogan led them down to the river and helped the marshal from his horse and made certain that he was settled before leaving. He left his horse with the marshal and made his way the few hundred yards to the canyon on foot, keeping in the cover of the trees just in case Grant Philips was watching.

Brogan crouched behind a large boulder some twenty or thirty yards from the canyon and studied hard, all the time listening for any unusual sounds.

At that point, to the left of the canyon, the wall of rock rose sheer for at least a hundred feet and swept to the left of the entrance for about four or five hundred yards where it became lost amongst the trees. The river, only about twenty feet wide, had carved a hollow beneath the overhanging rock creating a deep pool and, since Brogan could not swim, he gave up any idea of crossing and attempting to climb the rock.

To the right the ground rose steeply, but looked fairly easy to climb and seemed to end at the top of sheer wall, about thirty feet. Apart from the narrow trail which followed alongside the river through the canyon, there did not seem to be any other way. He stayed where he was for some time, looking and listening but failed to detect any sign of anyone waiting or hiding.

Keeping amongst the trees and well away from the trail, Brogan slowly made his way up the slope, only to discover that he had to scale a rock face some fifteen feet high. Taking the chance that Grant Philips was not in sight, he threw his rifle to the top of the rock face and proceeded to climb.

A few minutes later he was retrieving his rifle and briefly checking for any damage but found none. From that point onwards his caution and senses were on full alert, knowing that at any moment he was quite likely to simply stumble across anyone waiting.

From below, in the canyon, the top of the wall of rock gave the impression that the land above was fairly flat and tree covered. It was covered in trees but it proved to be far from flat. Apart from a very narrow band at the edge of the canyon about ten feet wide, the ground rose very steeply and was quickly lost in the forest. However, this was the route Brogan chose to follow.

The trees were packed together and made progress both easy and difficult. It was easy in the sense that footholds were readily available on the otherwise slippery, pine needle-littered floor but difficult in the sense that they were sometimes so closely packed that squeezing between them was something of an ordeal. The result was that progress was very slow and after ten minutes Brogan looked back only to realize that he had only travelled about fifty yards.

His progress was also slowed down by the fact that he had to constantly stop, look and listen. After about half an hour he began to wonder if Grant Philips was there.

A short time later Brogan came across another hazard, the crossing of which would present an easy target to anyone on the other side.

At some time in the fairly recent past there had been a land slip. A gap about fifty or sixty feet had been cut down the now very steep slope above him, stretching upwards for what appeared to be about 2,000 feet. A few shattered trees protruded through the scree and there were one or two fairly large boulders, but most of the scree consisted of broken rock no larger than a man's head with the vast majority being much smaller.

About half-way across, directly in front of Brogan, the remains of what had been a large tree seemed to be shooting out of the rubble but held in position by what was plainly a solid outcrop of rock. The scree appeared to flow around the outcrop and Brogan decided that this was to be the first point he would head for.

Below him it appeared that the avalanche had come to rest just before it reached the canyon as there were two trees standing untouched and not quite surrounded by the scree. Brogan waited, watched and listened for a few minutes before deciding that he had to take the chance and make a dash for the broken tree and the outcrop.

Reaching his target proved fairly easy if a little painful as his feet slithered on the loose stone causing him to fall and graze his legs and arms three times. However, he reached the outcrop without apparently being seen and he spent a good few minutes cleaning up a couple of deep scratches.

Once more, after attending his wounds, Brogan looked and listened but again he detected nothing although his brain was screaming out that there was danger ahead. Normally Brogan would listen to his gut feelings, but at that precise moment he was not in a position to find an alternative route: he had committed himself.

There was only about another thirty feet to go before he would be in the safe cover of the trees again but that thirty feet seemed more like three thousand. He edged himself around the shattered trunk of the tree, paused briefly to take one final look and to listen for the faintest hint and all seemed clear. Once more he crouched as best he could so as to reduce the target for anyone watching and tried to dash across the scree. He fell once, he could remember that and he seemed to remember falling a second time. A solid looking piece of rock turned out to be not so solid or secure, his ankle twisted, his foot slipped and his body lurched to one side....

It appeared to be raining, at least Brogan was conscious of feeling very wet. His eyes opened briefly but he had to close them as the rain simply poured into his face. He tried to move his arms and, although he could, the pain forced him to abandon the effort for a time. He was able to move one leg although it felt very painful. His other leg, the right, refused to move at all and he eventually realized that his ankle was firmly wedged in something.

He suddenly realized that he was holding something and painfully raised his right arm. The sight of what he was holding made him smile briefly – he had somehow managed to hold on to his rifle. The rain continued to pour down and, after some time, he had no idea how long, he was able to move his arms with comparative freedom although with considerable pain.

Slowly he managed to attain a sitting position and as he did so the rain suddenly stopped. He looked up into a cloudless sky, looked puzzled for a moment and then glanced behind him. Once again a brief smile flashed across his face as he saw that he had in fact been lying with his head under a small trickle of water as it drained off the mountain. His body was wet because the water had run down it. He glanced to his left and suddenly froze.

He was sitting on the edge of a sheer drop down into the canyon, perhaps some forty feet, not all that far but far enough to kill him. It appeared to have been his right ankle which had saved him from the final drop. He could now see that it was wedged, painfully so, amongst the exposed roots of a tree. Gingerly he felt the ankle and his leg and breathed a sigh of relief as he decided that there was nothing broken, although he had no doubt that the ankle would prove painful for some time.

Extracting his foot from the roots proved rather more difficult and certainly a lot more painful than he had expected but eventually he was free and standing to test his weight on the injury. Whilst he was still convinced that it was not broken, he knew that it had been severely twisted and bruised. He looked at where he was, at the base of the scree and on the edge of the canyon and then at the way ahead.

'No chance!' he said to himself, shaking his head a little sadly. 'There ain't no way I'm gonna be able to make it along there on this foot.'

'OK, so what do you do now?' he asked himself as was quite normal.

'Go back!' he answered himself.

'How? It's just as bad back that way as goin' ahead.'

'That's true!' He looked over the edge of the canyon and on to the flat, inviting trail below. 'We could go down.'

'Reckon you could?'

'Sure, why not? It looks an easy climb an' a few

more cuts an' bruises ain't gonna matter that much.'

'OK, let's go!'

The most painful and potentially the most dangerous part of the operation was actually lowering himself over the edge and he had to feel with his feet for some time before finding a hold. Before attempting the descent, he had wrapped his faithful Winchester in his now very tattered jacket, tied the arms securely and dropped it over the edge onto the trail below. The precious parcel seemed to survive the fall.

Very slowly and in great pain, Brogan inched his way down the cliff face, pausing quite often to gain his breath, ease his discomfort and pain and to look for finger and toe holds. A couple of times he began to question the wisdom of choosing to climb down, but he had started and there was now very little else he could do. The whole descent took him, he estimated, about half an hour but he was eventually on solid ground and feeling very sore and tired. He looked at the small river flowing alongside, at his own dirty, beaten and bloodied appearance and suddenly decided, rather against his natural instinct of avoiding baths, to immerse himself in the brown waters of the river.

Despite not liking getting his body wet, he had to confess that just lying in the cold water seemed to wash away some of his aches and pains. In fact he must have spent at least ten minutes simply lying there. Eventually he sat up and splashed water into his hair and rubbed vigorously, wincing a few times as either water or his fingers dug into various cuts. After having cleaned out those cuts and bruises he could see, he staggered back to the trail, picked up his jacket and rifle, decided that the jacket was just not worth bothering with and cast it to one side after checking the contents of the pockets.

Despite searching both jacket and his other pockets at least three times, there was no sign of his $340 and he sighed and looked up at the top of the canyon. The other contents were a small coil of thin wire and a length of twine both of which he could not recall ever needing.

Brogan was like that. He rarely threw anything away, always convincing himself that he might find a use for it one day. The twine and wire were stuffed into the back pocket of his jeans, where he discovered an ancient wad of chewing tobacco. The missing money troubled him greatly, something was not right. Half the plug ended up in his mouth and, after chewing at it for only a few seconds was spat out into the river to be followed by the unchewed half.

'Bloody awful!' he grunted. 'Guess I had it too long. Yeh, I guess at least a year is a mite long.'

After examining his Winchester and satisfying himself that it was undamaged, he gazed briefly up the wall of the canyon he had climbed down, decided that the climb was impossible and then thought about just what the hell he was doing there anyhow. There seemed little point in attempting to either find or expect to take or kill Deputy Marshal Grant Philips. The only way he could possibly achieve that result would be to climb back to the top of the canyon again. He looked at the climb again, remembered his aches and pains and shook his head.

'Fox ain't gonna be too pleased,' he said to himself, 'but who the hell cares if he's pleased or not? We'll just have to find some other way round.'

In actual fact Brogan discovered that he was further into the canyon than he had estimated. His original estimate of the length of the canyon was about half a mile, but he was quite certain that he had walked at least that distance before reaching the end. All the time he had been walking he had also been listening, but apart from normal sounds of running water, birds and the occasional sound of a forest animal, there was nothing.

At the same time he had been thinking about what to do with the injured Ebenezer Fox. It was plain to Brogan that the marshal had lost a lot of blood and the injury to the chest was very serious. Brogan suspected that many other men would have succumbed to such a serious injury and that the only thing which had kept Fox going was his own determination not to be outdone by his former assistants. Brogan also knew that unless he could get the marshal to a doctor quickly, even his cussedness and determination would not be enough.

He was also beginning to think that perhaps it might not be such a bad idea if a doctor were to look at him. One or two of his cuts were deep and really needed stitching and he was also beginning to question whether his ankle was broken or not. It was becoming increasingly painful to walk on.

A few yards out from the canyon, heading for the spot he had left the marshal, Brogan suddenly stopped, held his breath and listened keenly. The accident might have inflicted injuries upon his body but his senses were alert as ever....

TEN

Voices! Yes, definitely voices, one of them quite animated and most decidedly not that of Ebenezer Fox. Instinctively Brogan knew to whom the animated voice belonged, it could only be Grant Philips.

'Liar!' Brogan heard Philips shout. 'You cooked up some deal between you, a man just don't do things like that.'

It did not need a clairvoyant to tell Brogan exactly what the pair were talking about. Brogan could not help but smile and he crept forward, his Winchester clasped in rather painful hands, but he felt that he could use it effectively if he had to and it seemed highly likely that he would need to.

It seemed quite obvious that he was not expected, that Grant Philips must have either witnessed or come across Brogan's mishap. His thoughts immediately turned to the money missing from his pocket but he did wonder why he had not been killed.

The scene by the river was pretty much as Brogan had expected as he crouched behind a large rock. Grant Philips was standing over the

140

body of Marshal Fox, his rifle held menacingly close to the injured man's head. Philips appeared to be doing most of the talking, although there must have been a few weak words from the marshal but Brogan could not hear them.

'You got one last chance, Ebenezer,' grated Philips, 'tell me what you've done with the money an' I'll let you live. By the look of you the chances are you're goin' to die anyhow.'

This time Brogan did hear the marshal speak. 'I told you, he gave it to the orphanage! Why the hell can't you get it through that thick head of yours that I'm tellin' the truth?'

'I know you, Ebenezer,' growled Philips. 'You want the money for yourself. You got one minute then I'm goin' to blow your brains out.'

'He's tellin' the truth!' Brogan's voice echoed around the rocks. He had been unable to get a clear shot at Philips.

Grant Philips swung his rifle in the general direction of Brogan's voice and fired, well wide of his intended target. 'You're dead!' shouted the deputy as he crouched, using the marshal as cover. 'I seen your body, I felt your heart, you was definitely dead!'

'Then you'd better believe I'm a ghost!' called Brogan. 'I guessed it must've been you who took what money I did have.'

'You sure didn't need it! OK, McNally, so you ain't dead yet but you will be pretty soon. You was sure cut up bad, maybe I should've made sure.'

'You had your chance!' laughed Brogan. 'That's the trouble with folk like you, you don't make sure when you have the chance.'

'I don't know what deal you an' Ebenezer cooked up between you,' called Philips, 'but I reckon I've got the upper hand right now. You want him alive, you do just like I say or else my next shot blows his brains out.'

'Go ahead!' invited Brogan. 'There ain't no deal between us; I really couldn't care less what the hell happens to him. Why should I?'

'You tell me!' Philips shouted again. 'OK, so you don't give a damn abut him. What is it you do want? Why the hell was you tryin' to get him back to Nelson?'

'That's a question I keep askin' myself!' replied Brogan. 'So far I ain't come up with no sensible answer. Go ahead, kill him but you do that an' you've lost your cover.'

Grant Philips was obviously thinking about this and he whispered something to the marshal. Fox just laughed and called out to Brogan.

'Take no heed of him, McNally. It looks like I'm a goner anyhow, at least a bullet would get it over an' done with quick.'

'Bastard!' snarled Philips. 'Come on damn you, on your feet!'

Making sure that the marshal was between him and Brogan, Philips hauled him to his feet. 'OK, McNally, this time you win but you'd better make sure you don't turn your back, not even for a second 'cos you just might feel a bullet in it.'

'I got eyes up my ass, remember!' laughed Brogan.

Although he was ready to shoot and had the

marshal in his sights, Brogan was unable to get a clear shot at Grant Philips. Using the marshal as a shield, Philips slowly backed off towards his horse, which he then led, still using the marshal as a shield, away from the river towards the trees. Only when he was among the trees did he suddenly let the marshal go. There was a very brief instant when, had Brogan's hands not been quite so stiff, he could have shot Philips but the moment was past almost as soon as it presented itself.

Ebenezer Fox fell to the ground and Philips was lost to sight. Brogan did not move straight away, wary that Grant Philips was still close by and ready for any move. Ten minutes passed during which time Brogan detected a disturbance further along the trail and decided that Philips had made good his escape. Even so, it was with great caution that he made his way to the injured marshal.

Ebenezer Fox was not dead, but he was certainly unconscious and looking very ashen. Brogan realized that time was running out very quickly and that help for the marshal was an absolute priority. He had very serious doubts as to whether Ebenezer could survive a prolonged ride and the chances of his reaching Nelson City that day were nil.

The only logical solution seemed to be that he had to leave the marshal somewhere safe and ride into town himself and take the doctor to the marshal. However, with Grant Philips on the loose, he would almost certainly finish off the marshal if he came across him. Brogan decided that he had no alternative but to force the marshal on to his horse and look for a more secure place to hide him.

Getting Ebenezer on to his horse was not easy, every movement seemed to bring forth fresh blood from his wound, blood he could ill afford to lose. However, he was eventually up and strapped on to the saddle and, after hauling the body of Walter Jefferson on to the other horse, Brogan led the way through the canyon.

He had half expected trouble from Grant Philips but the crossroads were reached without any problem. It had been Brogan's intention to head straight for Nelson City but something, he did not know what, made him take the trail towards the south-west and Brandon.

Darkness was drawing rapidly, the sun now obscured and well below the tree line when he saw it. Nothing more than a very brief flash of light about a hundred yards off the trail amongst the trees. It was very little but it offered the only hope of any help for the marshal. About fifty yards further on Brogan came across a path cut through the forest.

The path led, as Brogan had hoped and almost expected, to a solitary log cabin which, judging by the large number of animal pelts and skins he could just make out stretched across frames, Brogan assumed belonged to a trapper.

Long before he had reached the cabin, his approach had been detected by a large, snarling dog which now barred his way. Brogan reined to halt and patted his horse's neck to calm her. Two minutes later a large, bearded man came towards them from the cabin, hunting rifle at the ready, a long-barrelled contraption which Broan knew could easily blow him apart from fifty yards.

'Yeh?' slurped the hunter, spitting on to the ground. 'What the hell do you want here?'

'A doctor,' replied Brogan. 'I got me an injured man here what needs a doctor real bad.'

'Ain't no doctor here,' said the man stating the obvious. 'Nearest is in Nelson City. You gotta take him there.' He moved slowly round and looked at the body of Walter Jefferson. 'Him?' he grunted.

'Dead,' replied Brogan. 'Look, I know you ain't got no doctor here, but the marshal just ain't goin' to make it to Nelson. I need somewheres to let him rest while I go fetch the doctor.'

'Marshal?' asked the man, raising a hairy eyebrow a little.

'Ebenezer Fox,' replied Brogan. 'Other one is … was … his deputy, Walter Jefferson.'

The hunter once again spat on the ground and moved towards the marshal. 'Bastard!' he growled. 'By rights I ought to tell you to get the hell out of it an' hope the bastard dies.'

'Are you?'

The hunter thought about it for a few moments. 'Naw, guess not,' he said eventually. 'He ain't done me no harm, but there ain't a single soul in the county what wouldn't like to see his dead body. OK, you can bring him inside, my woman knows about these things, she'll do what she can.' He shouted at the dog who grudgingly and snarlingly cowered in the undergrowth at the side of the track and Brogan led the other two horses warily past it, expecting it to leap out and snap at the horses' legs. However, it did not and quietened down almost as soon as they were past.

The hunter's woman turned out to be a rather large Indian squaw whom Brogan recognized as being of the Crow tribe. He knew only one word of Crow and that was the word for peace. She seemed quite impressed when he used it and immediately assumed he could speak fluent Crow. When she discovered that he could not, she simply laughed.

Marshal Fox was carried into the single-roomed cabin and laid on the floor close to the fire. Immediately the woman set to removing his clothes to examine the wound. She grunted something and the hunter reached for a large bottle standing in a corner.

'Don't know what the hell she puts in that stuff,' he said, 'but it's guaranteed to cure anythin'. I ain't gonna ask what the hell's been goin' on, it ain't none of my business. If anyone can save your friend, she can. Marvellous woman, best one I ever had.'

'He ain't no friend of mine,' said Brogan. 'In fact he tried to kill me, but I guess you could say I owe him in some way.'

'You know your own business!' declared the hunter. 'What about the other one?'

'He tried to kill me too,' said Brogan. 'In fact there's another one out there somewhere who wants to kill us both.'

'Nice friends you have,' grunted the hunter. 'What the hell brought you this way?'

'Dunno,' admitted Brogan, 'just a gut feelin'. How far is it to Nelson from here?'

'Maybe twenty miles, I don't know for sure. Best way is straight through the forest, which is OK if you know it an' then in daylight. You ain't figurin' on tryin' to make it now are you? The forest ain't no place for a man what don't know it at night.'

'I'm used to forests at night,' said Brogan a little boastfully. 'He needs a doctor pretty damned quick.'

The hunter shook his head, obviously confused. 'I don't get it. You shoot a man so bad he's liable to die an' then you want to get him to a doctor....'

'I didn't shoot him,' corrected Brogan, 'one of his deputies did.'

'I heard about them, Jefferson an' Philips, real mean bastards. I still don't get it. Why should he try to kill you an' his deputies try to kill you both?'

Brogan laughed. 'It'd take too long to explain. Thing is I gotta get to Nelson as quick as I can so's I can fetch the doctor.'

'You don't go nowhere before I look at you!' declared the woman, standing up and roughly pulling at Brogan's shirt. 'You hurt pretty bad too, this one need stitch, this one too.' She prodded two deep cuts which made Brogan wince.

'I'll be OK,' assured Brogan, not relishing the thought of the squaw trying to stitch his wounds.

'You do like you told!' scolded the woman producing a knife and suddenly ripping Brogan's shirt apart. 'See, plenty more, some need stitch, some no.' She nodded at the hunter who swept a large table clear with one sweep of his huge arm. 'You lie down....' She pushed Brogan towards the table. 'I stitch.'

'Hell, ma'am,' Brogan tried to protest, 'it's OK, I'll be fine, I had worse before.'

'Don't be fright!' laughed the squaw. 'I stitch very good, I do it many times. It no hurt.'

Brogan was not at all sure about it not hurting but he felt himself being forced on to the table where his few remaining clothes were ripped off leaving him naked. The squaw made some laughing comment to the hunter and he passed her the bottle of cure-all which she splashed on to the various wounds. Brogan winced as the liquid coursed into the cuts, but it seemed to deaden the pain. The next thing he knew a curved needle had been produced, threaded with what looked like thin twine and the task of stitching commenced.

Brogan had to confess that there was very little pain and within ten minutes the squaw stood back to admire her handiwork. He was allowed to get off the table and the hunter appeared with some clean clothes which fitted him almost perfectly.

'Yours?' he asked the hunter.

'Naw,' he drawled, 'used to belong to my son, but he won't be needin' 'em no more, he died last year.'

'Sorry to hear that,' said Brogan as a matter of course.

'Moose gored him,' said the hunter. 'His own fault, I warned him but he took no notice. OK, that's you done. What you do now is up to you.'

'I reckon the marshal still needs a doctor,' said Brogan. 'No disrespect to you or your woman, but he's goin' to need a bit more than your medicine an' a bit of stitchin'.'

'Maybe you're right,' agreed the hunter. 'You ain't thinkin' of startin' out now though?'

'The sooner I start the sooner the doctor gets here,' said Brogan.

'You no fit to ride!' said the squaw. 'You rest tonight.'

'Thanks, but no thanks,' said Brogan. 'I guess I owe him in some way. I'll be OK.'

'Your funeral,' said the hunter.

Brogan decided to ignore the hunter's directions and returned along the trail to the crossroads where he turned towards Nelson City. He guessed that it must have been almost midnight and he doubted if he would have any trouble from Grant Philips. He was having some discomfort from the rough and ready surgery performed by the squaw and one or two of the wounds were beginning to ooze some blood. He wondered if he should have listened to the squaw but then decided that he had suffered worse in the past and would survive.

Progress was very slow, partly because of the almost total blackness and partly because anything faster than his old horse ambling along at other than her normal slow walk simply served to make his wounds ooze more blood and create a great deal of pain. However, he reached Nelson City just as dawn was breaking.

The Nelson City sheriff's office was his first call,

rather to the annoyance of the sheriff. He listened to Brogan's story with a great deal of suspicion but eventually decided that this strange saddle tramp was telling the truth. He directed Brogan a few doors along the street to the office of Doctor James Harris, MD.

Doc Harris too listened to what Brogan had to say with great suspicion which only seemed to be allayed when he insisted on examining Brogan's wounds. He prodded and grunted and occasionally shook his head, but he did not attempt to repair what he obviously considered rather shoddy work.

'Must've thought she was stitchin' hides!' he commented. 'Mind, I must confess that that medicine of hers is real powerful stuff, I use it myself but she won't let on how to make it. No, it could be that she did the best thing, there's some nasty cuts there and they could easily have started to go bad by now. It ain't pretty work but it's sure effective.'

'What about Ebenezer Fox?' asked Brogan.

'From what you tell me he sounds in a bad way,' said the doc. 'Little Bird will do her best for him though....'

'Little Bird!' exclaimed Brogan. 'She sure don't look like no little bird.'

'I guess she must've once,' grinned Doc Harris. 'OK, I guess I'll just have to go out there an' see what I can do for Ebenezer. Mind, there's a good many who wouldn't be too bothered if he died.'

'Includin' you?' asked Brogan.

The doc shrugged. 'I ain't got no quarrel with

the man, I guess he's only doin' his job. Don't worry, I'll do everythin' I can for him. Are you comin' back with me?'

'I ain't had no sleep last night,' said Brogan, 'but I reckon I've gone past it now. Sure, I'll go with you.'

'Then we might as well start out now,' said the doc. 'We might make it by midday.'

Doc Harris was not far out in his estimation, they reached the hunter's cabin about half an hour after midday. The dog snarled and barred their way but was quickly and efficiently dealt with by the squaw, Little Bird. The dog disappeared, still growling, into the forest.

'Where's Trapper?' Doc Harris asked Little Bird.

'He go check a few traps,' said Little Bird. 'You no come to see Trapper, he very fine. Marshal Fox, he not so fine.'

'Let's take a look,' sighed the doc.

They were led into the cabin where Ebenezer Fox was still on the floor close to the fire and looking very much worse than when Brogan had last seen him. Doc Harris examined the wound to his chest, grunted and looked briefly at the wound to his leg.

'That'll wait a bit,' he said; 'looks like the leg's broke and the bullet's still in there. I can deal with that easy enough. His chest is another matter. I'd say there was a bullet lodged in his lung. I'm goin' to have to do some diggin'.'

'Will he survive?' asked Brogan.

'I can get the bullet out an' clean him up,' said the doc. 'After that it's up to him. He's a determined old cuss but I think he's goin' to need all the determination he's got an' a bit more besides.'

Ebenezer Fox, although not unconscious, was plainly not really aware of what was happening around him. Doc Harris asked Brogan and Little Bird to lift the marshal on to the large table, where Little Bird stripped off his clothes.

Little Bird wiped away most of the congealed blood and Doc Harris gazed into the wound, prodding and lifting and mumbling to himself. Little Bird too seem completely fascinated and lost in the operation. Brogan, although not at all squeamish about such things, felt that he was simply in the way and decided to go outside.

There was no sign of Trapper, the hunter, nor of the dog and Brogan was quite thankful for that since there was nobody about to control the animal should it decide to attack him. He settled down on a pile of logs to await the completion of the operation now taking place inside the cabin.

Brogan was awake! He did not move except to open his eyes and swiftly scan his surroundings. There was still no sign of Trapper nor of the dog but he did not think that either had returned. If they had he felt certain that he would have been alerted. However, now he was awake and his senses told him that all was not as it should be.

He did not move for several minutes, all the time looking and listening but whatever it was that had alerted him did not make its presence heard, only felt. Eventually, very slowly and with apparent casualness, he stood up and ambled slowly across to his horse and slipped his Winchester out of the saddle holster. He returned to the cabin and looked in just to make certain that Trapper had not returned. Doc Harris and Little Bird were still hunched over the body of Ebenezer Fox and both seemed completely oblivious to Brogan. As expected that was no sign of Trapper.

Brogan went outside and sat on the log pile for some time and was beginning to wonder if he had imagined the whole thing. The sounds of the forest all seemed quite normal, bird activity was pretty much as he would have expected and even his old horse, who normally sensed things, seemed quite content as she chewed at a bale of hay.

'Must be gettin' old,' he muttered to himself. 'Maybe I am, maybe I'm not, but I still got this feelin' that somethin' ain't right out there.'

He sighed and slowly wandered down the track, watching and listening but neither seeing nor hearing anything unusual. He had just about convinced himself that his mind was playing tricks and as a result his guard dropped. An action he immediately regretted.

'Just keep that rifle down an' turn round real slow!' came the command. Brogan mentally cursed himself but was not so foolish as to attempt to outgun the voice he recognized as Grant Philips'. He turned to find Philips about twenty yards away, his rifle aimed steadily. 'I said I'd get you, you bastard!' grated Philips. 'Well now I've got you. What's goin' on inside the cabin?'

'Doc Harris is operatin' on Ebenezer,' said Brogan.

'Doc Harris!' grunted Philips, plainly surprised. 'Pity about that 'cos he's wastin' his time tryin' to save old Ebenezer. It's a pity but it looks like I'm goin' to have to kill him too.'

'An' what good will that do you?' asked Brogan.

'Oh, I got it all worked out,' replied Philips. 'It's just a pity you had to bring the doc in. You've already killed Walter Jefferson an' tried to kill Ebenezer. I took him to Trapper's cabin, called Doc Harris in then you turned up again, killed Ebenezer, Trapper an' that squaw of his an' then Doc Harris. You didn't manage to kill me though an' I killed you.'

'An' you become the hero!' laughed Brogan. 'It could be that most of Nelson City knows I fetched Doc Harris by now. Even if most don't know, the sheriff an' Mrs Harris sure do.'

'The sheriff!' grated Philips. 'You're kiddin' me, old Marty Thornton don't get up in the middle of the night for nobody.'

'OK, so don't believe me,' shrugged Brogan; 'you just go ahead an' see what happens.'

Grant Philips was obviously unsure and shuffled slightly but his rifle remained steadily aimed at Brogan. There was a slight movement on the edge of the forest close to Philips but he did not seem to notice it. Brogan moved to one side slightly so as to turn Philips' back to the forest.

'Stay where you are!' rasped Philips.

'What for?' smiled Brogan. 'Since you is goin' to kill me anyhow, it don't make no difference.'

Grant Philips tensed himself and muttered, 'Bastard!'

Brogan never actually saw the dog leap. One second Grant Philips was about to shoot and the next second his shot had gone aimlessly into the air as he howled and struggled under the snarling mass of muscle, sinew and teeth.

Suddenly Trapper was also pulling and hitting the dog with his rifle butt although fierce as the blows were, they seemed to have little effect. Brogan too ran forward to lend his weight to the struggle. All the time Grant Philips screamed in agony.

Philips and the dog fell to the ground, both Trapper and Brogan doing their best to beat off the animal but the beast was too crazed to even feel anything. There was a sudden, horrific scream as the dog managed to get on top of Philips, followed by a single shot.

Brogan looked up to see Trapper still pointing his rifle at the dog which had given a brief whimper and was now slumped across the bloodied and torn body of Grant Philips. Brogan sighed and pulled the dog off the body. It was not a pretty sight; Grant Philips was obviously dead, his throat having been torn apart leaving his head almost severed.

'Allus knew that dog'd do for somebody one day,' rasped Trapper, lowering his gun. 'Won't do it no more though.'

By this time Doc Harris and Little Bird had dashed from the house. Little Bird seemed more concerned about the dog than anyone else but Doc Harris immediately examined Grant Philips and very quickly confirmed what both Brogan and Trapper knew, that Philips was dead.

Three days later Brogan was once again leaving Nelson City. Marshal Ebenezer Fox had recovered sufficiently to confirm Brogan's story – apart from the part about his trying to kill Brogan, which Brogan too had left unsaid. Brogan had removed his money from Grant Philips shortly after he had been killed. Doc Harris had confirmed the attack by the dog almost as if he had witnessed the whole thing. Brogan's wounds had been treated again but he ignored advice to remain in town until he was fully recovered.

'Well, old girl,' Brogan said to his horse. 'Looks like we cheated Old Man Death again, three times. He's gettin' closer though; a few years ago he'd never have got that close. We'll just have to learn to take to easy.'

The horse nodded and neighed her full agreement.